LIGHTSTORM

Peter Hamilton began writing short stories in 1987 for various magazines and anthologies, but has been writing critically acclaimed adult science-fiction novels full-time for Pan Books since 1993. This is his first children's book, and novel for Orion. He lives near Rutland Water.

For more information about the books,
competitions and activities, check out our website:
http://www.orionbooks.co.uk/web

THEWEB
LIGHTSTORM

◆

PETER F. HAMILTON

Dolphin Paperbacks

First published in Great Britain in 1998
as a Dolphin paperback
by Orion Children's Books
a division of the Orion Publishing Group Ltd
Orion House
5 Upper St Martin's Lane
London WC2H 9EA

A catalogue record for this book is available from the British Library

Typeset by Deltatype Ltd, Birkenhead, Merseyside
Printed in Great Britain by Clays Ltd, St Ives plc

ISBN 1 85881 550 9 (pb)

CONTENTS

CHAPTER ONE

MEETING OFF
SUNSET

I was flying down Sunset Boulevard, three metres above the ground, flapping my wings in a lazy motion as if I were part of a slow-motion scene in some old 2-D movie. It's a deceptive action, I was actually zipping along quite fast above the heads of the historical characters and myth-creatures thronging the wide yellow-brick strand between the Hollywood gamer company blocks. Good thing, too. I didn't want to keep my news exclusive. What happened last night was plain creepy.

Up ahead, a group of tall elves and knights, wearing armour that shone like polished chrome, were standing outside the MaxiFox block. They were waiting to spin in to the *Camelot Orc Attack* site. From my angle the surface of the block looked like a chrome rainbow that was slowly melting into whirlpool curves. A big rosette of sapphire and emerald slid down in front of the group, and they stepped through together.

They couldn't have been phreaks. The Camelot games were venomous when they started coming out. That was months ago. Now, everyone knows the blackwire tricks to boost your play character status. Perhaps they were one-mip nostalgia buffs, a bit like Grandpa. Except he's not one-mip. Of course!

I flew on past the MaxiFox block, with its paltry queue of people waiting to spin in. They really ought to shove *Camelot* out on disk and reboot the block. It's November, after all; the gamer companies are starting to line up their big new Christmas titles.

Disney's block was already advertising the new Schwarzenegger game with sleek, flying V-shaped starships launch-
ing from its roof in a roar of sparkling afterburner flame.
Just watching them vanish into the blue sky made you
want to join the colonists they were taking to new worlds.
Well, it did me anyway. Spielberg's block was orbited by
amazing intergalactic vortex holes blinking open for its
Dark Powers game. I zipped underneath one and did a full
roll so I could look up into it. If you're fast enough you can
catch a good glimpse of the promo scenes they reveal.

Most of the companies had taken space as *the* theme this
year, what with the Mars landing in two days time. I loved
it. Christmas for twelve solid months.

I'm going to be an astronaut when I'm older. Yeah, I
know, you've heard that one before. But with me its
bottom-line real. I've wanted it ever since I gave up on the
idea of being a bird warden down at the marsh sanctuary.
That was when I was about seven, and realized just how
dirty the job would be, wriggling round in all that mud to
rescue the strange, bewildered birds the weather brings in
from Africa and Asia these days. So I've concentrated on
getting the kind of grade ratings on my school science
courses that the Global Space Agency is looking for. Just
another seven years, including university, to go, and I'll be
eligible to apply to GSA for full training. I'm already a
registered cadet with them.

The Tropicana site is in a block past the last of the
gamers. I flew straight in. The spin put me above a beach of
scarlet sand with a skyline that was just fading to twilight.
It was busy, the clusters of white café chairs crowding above
the water line were nearly all taken.

As the Tropicana is a contact and leisure site, all the
avatars inside were human-form. But my computer is
loaded with an EC licensed Equal Access User program, so I
could keep my bird-form. It's shaped like a manta, but with
silvery blue skin and a pterodactyl head. The sense of
freedom it gives me during flight is fabulous. I suppose it
must be similar to the zero-G which astronauts experience.

I circled round till I found an empty table, then settled beside it. My friends started to spin in after a couple of minutes. About time! I was getting impatient.

Selim was first, using his direct site access program. A shimmering vortex hole materialized above the table, and a purple egg-shaped landing pod popped out. It landed on the sand beside me. The upper half hinged open to show a cockpit with a control console that was all switches and flashing lights. Selim climbed out of the ejector seat and grinned.

His avatar is a boy about my age, thirteen, average height and weight, but with the sort of features that are as regular as only a program can conjure up (plus skin that doesn't have a single spot!).

'Hi, Aynsley,' he said. 'So, what's the hot fly you've got for us?'

'I'll tell you when the others get here. I'd just have to repeat it every time, else.'

He stuck his tongue out. It was a long strip of wet flesh that licked round in front of his face. Neat upgrade!

Drunlo was next to arrive. A wooden trapdoor flipped up from the beach, showering sand everywhere. He climbed up a ladder from what looked like a stone cellar with flaming torches on the wall. As always his avatar was an eleven-year-old, though he was in his standard medieval urchin clothes.

Bayliss and Katie turned up together, walking across the sand. He's the only one of us who doesn't bother with an avatar image; his realoe showed us a chubby face with a brow that seemed to be permanently frowning. Katie's avatar was Rebecca Ryan; this year's *Access On* hostess. Sixteen years old. An easy smile that produces dimples everywhere, every time. Legs almost slimmer than her arms, and twice as long. So perfect she could be be an avatar program herself.

'It was there again last night,' I told them. 'I saw it three times. Bigger than before. Brighter, too.'

'That's it?' Selim asked. He was really withering about it,

too. 'That's your fly? You saw lights out over the marsh? Honestly, Aynsley, we can hardly chase this fade. They're called will-o'-the-wisp. Browse your encyclopaedia, it's just gas that's given off from decaying plants. Methane, like farts.'

'This isn't a will-o'-the-wisp,' I said hotly. 'You think I don't know what a will-o'-the-wisp is? I've lived by the marsh for ten years. I've *seen* them. They're pale, like a glowing mist. This is different. It's ... it's a *lightstorm*. Every time it's like a bubble of light that erupts out of the ground then just vanishes. And it never happens twice in the same place. Least, not yet.'

'What do you think it is?' Katie asked.

'I don't know.'

'Flying saucers taking off,' Selim suggested.

'Don't be silly,' Bayliss told him.

I'd been sort of relying on Bayliss for support. His science grades make me look like a one-mip by comparison. That's how we met, surfing round the GSA Olympus mission site. I was accessing the crew member who was in the provider suit that day. Bayliss was interested in the results from the ship's gamma ray telescope.

'I'm not,' Selim protested. 'How can you say it's silly? We're landing people on Mars in two days time. Why is aliens landing here so improbable?'

'It's not improbable, just very unlikely. Besides, Aynsley said it was just bubbles of light not whole ships.'

'OK, then it's their exhaust jets he's seeing, and the saucers themselves use stealth technology like our air force fighters.'

'If it is any sort of aircraft, then it's likely to be a secret military one.'

'I don't think so,' I said. 'Not using the marshes. It's a registered nature reserve area, and the village is only a couple of kilometres away. That's not being very secret, is it?'

'So what do you think it is?' Katie asked, again.

'I really don't know. That's why I wanted to bring you in

to help. The first time I saw the lights I thought it was interesting. Now I'm getting worried, because I don't understand them. I can't find an explanation in any educational text or memory file. That's really strange. I mean, we all know how to format a knowbot to browse public information sites, that's one-mip stuff. So why haven't I found out what it is? If it's natural, it has to be filed somewhere.' I could tell I'd got them curious, even Selim. Not *knowing* is terribly wrong in the information age. Our world is open to us. Or it should be. Having things hidden from the public belongs in the dark ages. Grandpa is always banging on about how awful life was when the only information people had came from the newspapers and television. Editors always chose what you could see or read based on what they thought was the most interesting or entertaining. Sort of like benign censorship, Grandpa says.

I don't know which upset me the most. The lightstorms themselves, or not being able to find out about them. Two things that shouldn't happen, somehow connected. It's like waking up to find the sky's turned green.

'I suppose we can all write a knowbot request for you,' Drunlo said. 'Those network librarians are getting really sophisticated, they should be able to track down any information providing you phrase the request correctly. Between us we ought to be able to find a bite on lightstorms. You might just have made a mistake formatting your request.'

I glared at him as well as my avatar characteristics would allow me. 'I don't believe I did.'

'You weren't spidered off a file were you?' Katie enquired. 'No.'

'What do the other people living beside the marsh say the lightstorms are?' Bayliss asked.

'I don't know,' I admitted. I knew that back in my cocoon I'd be blushing inside my Websuit. 'I haven't asked them.'

'Well, why not?' Selim said in exasperation.

Because I don't like any of them, they're not my friends,

and they enjoy making my life a misery. But I didn't say that out loud. 'Nobody else has seen them, yet. They're too far away, and no one really looks over the marsh at night.'

'Except you,' Selim said, with a short laugh.

'Hey, curl up,' Katie snapped. 'We are what we are. All of us. If you don't like us, spin out.'

'I didn't say that,' he answered. 'I'm just saying that not everyone spends their evenings looking out at marshes they can't see. I think it's a valid point.'

'Do you want to tell us?' Drunlo asked me cautiously.

'No big secret. I'm thinking of fitting a low-light amplifier to my telescope so I can watch the birds at night. It was a full moon last week, so I was scanning round the marshes to find out what I could see anyway. And that's when I saw a lightstorm for the first time.'

'This phenomenon could have been going on for quite a while then? Bayliss said. 'Ever since the marsh was renovated.'

'I suppose so. But the ecology crews finished that part of the nature restoration scheme two years ago. I think if it had been going on for that long someone would have seen it.'

'Quite right,' Katie said. 'It sounds to me as if this has only just started. I think you should report it, Aynsley.'

'Who to?'

'And what would he say is happening?' Bayliss said. 'We were sceptical about lights in the night, and we know Aynsley is honest with us. The local authorities would laugh him off their site.'

'What do we do then?'

'The obvious. Gather more information. Then when we have the facts we'll know what to do.'

'All right,' she said. 'I'll be happy to format a knowbot that'll browse for lightstorms.'

'We all should,' Bayliss said. 'And Aynsley.'

'Yes?'

'You'll have to go out into the marsh and scout round.'

'Why?' I tried to keep the consternation out of my voice.

It wasn't easy. Of course, he didn't know what he was asking. But I wasn't going to tell him that.

'So you can see if there is any evidence of what's been going on.' The tone was of someone stating the utterly obvious. 'Do you know roughly the area where these lightstorms have been appearing?'

'Er, yes, I suppose so.'

'Good. That's settled then. Each of us will find what we can this afternoon, and then meet back here this evening, usual time.'

CHAPTER TWO

MY FAMILY, AND
HOW TO SURVIVE THEM

A trip into the marsh! Why hadn't I just kept my big mouth shut? Worse, what was I thinking of, saying *yes*?

I suppose I told them because I wanted to be the centre of attention. People always want others to think they are interesting. It's the route to popularity. And let's face it, that's an empty file in my site.

Grandpa says people are always ridiculously competitive and paranoid from the moment they're born to when they die. He also says people are basically stupid.

I think he's right.

After I spun out of the Tropicana I took my suit off and slung it on my bed. No sign of the voms. Thankfully! I wasn't expecting any, I'd only been in for twenty minutes. Most mornings I spin in for a couple of hours at least, so Realworld and I aren't used to each other at this time of day. Nothing had changed in my cocoon. The walls are all covered in holoposters of various chunks of space hardware. Satellites and stations orbiting the Earth; a shuttle taking off from Cape Town; a survey team at work on the moon. There are pictures of birds, too; ordinary 2-D colour laser prints. I took most of them; I'm quite handy with a vid-snap camera. My latest posters are tacked up at the end of my bed, showing the Olympus ships sliding into orbit above Mars. A two-metre flatscreen next to the window runs text displays from mission control, keeping me constantly updated.

There's only a limited amount of space on my desk, so the computer tower has to sit on the floor to make room for my science projects. I've got a healthy selection of tools to help me assemble various card stacks to augment the tower functions. At the moment I'm trying to put together a stack that will automate my telescope.

It's a beautiful ash-grey tube over a metre long, very powerful. Dad gave it to me on a sort-of loan; he was quite a keen amateur astronomer when he was young. The trouble is, when it's set up on a tripod I find it difficult to reach the eyepiece. So if I can fix it up with actuators and a decent video camera I'll be able to lie on my bed and watch the images on the flatscreen.

That's why it's in my cocoon at the moment, rather than outside. And my window faces towards the marsh. See? That's how come I found the lightstorms. Most of life's events are accidents and coincidences all bunched up together, I suppose.

There was no one about when I went out. Typical for our house, everybody always doing their own thing. I ought to explain about my family; not that we're odd, or anything. No serial killers or sorceresses lurking in the attic. Well, not unless you count Uncle Elton, but we're not allowed to mention him because of where he is at the moment and what he did to get sent there. Apart from him we're almost cogs. My dad, Forrest Clemson, is a tax lawyer at a London-site partnership. Grandpa Donald is always accusing him of being a soulless corporate robot working for the forces of darkness. He says if rich companies paid more tax then Europe would have better social security and healthcare schemes, and Dad's the one who helps them avoid it. Grandpa likes to think that his side of the family are all romantic rebels. Dad always points out that the reason he and my mum, Marriane, met in the first place was because Grandpa sent her to the partnership so she wouldn't have to pay so much tax. You see, Mum used to be in a girls group that had a couple of hit albums around 2010. She sings really well and she wrote some of the group's songs, too. Being in the mediabiz is a bit like winning the lottery every week, apparently.

Mum doesn't sing these days, at least not in a group. Me and my younger brother Edwyn put an end to that career just by being born. She still writes music, though, for a company that provides incidental scores for games. She has her causes, too; she's a parish councillor, and on the board of the Norfolk Community Health Committee, and a school governor (which is awful, she knows both my supervisory teachers really well), and sits as an advisor for two local special needs charities.

It's good for people to have causes, to help others. Except … at times I wish she was just my mum and nothing else. But that's selfish. She did put a lot of what she made from the group into trust accounts for me and Edwyn. Not that I can get at it for ages; I just have to scrape by on this really small percentage of the monthly interest. Banks and trustees (Mum and Grandpa!) just don't understand how much money you need simply to survive in the modern world. I can only ever buy a hundredth of the stuff I want.

Actually, that's more than most kids my age get. I suppose I like Mum quite a lot really; even though she does worry and tries a little too hard.

The old mobile phone was fully charged, so I put it into my coat pocket before I went out. That's another thing Mum insists on if I'm outside by myself. I'll be able to call if I get into any difficulty.

I took the ramp down to the garden. Our house isn't actually a house in the ordinary sense. It's a boat in the middle of a field. We live just outside a village called Heacham, on a big field that runs along the rear of the beach. There are several wooden bunglaows sharing the field with us, as well as a few other boats. They used to be grain barges back in the last century, then after their working life was over someone dragged them ashore and turned them into homes.

It's utterly perfect during the summer. Well, most of the year, really. We're on the southern edge of the The Wash; that means the beach goes on for kilometres, and there are no cliffs, just a low bluff sprouting tufts of reed grass, so I can get down to it easily. The marshes begin at the end of the field, and they stretch along to the mouth of the River Ouse. A huge great zone of nothing. There are tourists in the summer, but not many. Grandpa says when he was young millions of people flew abroad for holidays, or drove down to Cornwall. I can't imagine what that was like. They say the Web's secure business sites put an end to commuter traffic; and the game sites killed off package holidays, along with the rise in the cost of aviation fuel. Petrol reached fifteen Euros a litre at its worst, which stopped any kind of driving apart from utterly essential journeys. Apparently, there are still a million private cars licensed in England (we have one of them), but now the rail network is being restored and expanded everyone who wants to travel uses trains and buses.

Some of the kids from the other bungalows were playing a football game on the grass between the row of buildings. I trundled past as fast as I could go without making it obvious I was in a rush to get away from them. With it being November I was wrapped up well; my canary-yellow wool coat, a long emerald scarf, and a grey bobble hat with ear flaps. Normally, they would have crowded round and had their fun; sneered at my clothes, demanded to know where I was going, what I was doing; make out they were astronauts in freefall. I've lost count of how many times my hats have been chucked on to the beach (always a long way from the path down) or dunked in the stream which runs along the back of the field. Sometimes, I think the Realworld conservatives are right and kids should be bundled off to school every day so they can develop social skills, or at least learn that other people have feelings. Experience has shown me how futile that hope is.

Today though, their zero-mip game was taking up their full attention. I got clear with just a few jeers and shouts.

Mr Griffin was pottering round his front garden, clipping back his scrawny fuchsia bushes. Both of his cats were curled up in a wicker chair on the veranda, watching him. 'Hello there, Aynsley,' he called as I went past his front gate. It's about the only part of his fence that is still standing.

'Hello.' I showed a bit, but didn't stop.

'So, what's new and groovy in that infernal electronic universe of yours, my boy?'

Groovy! Mr Griffin is approximately five hundred years old. He doesn't like the Web, which means he gets on great with Grandpa. 'The new Schwarzenegger is due for access in five days.'

He groaned loudly. 'Oh, good grief. I remember when acting dynasties meant Olivier and Richardson and Douglas. Schwarzenegger, tut tut.'

'It's not quite acting now, Mr Griffin. The sites are concepts.'

'Don't remind me. Heavens, my agent hasn't called for weeks, simply weeks.'

'I'm sorry.' Mr Griffin is an actor. Too old to retrain when Hollywood switched from films to games, and TV abandoned drama series, he said. Lots of adults in this country still enjoy going to the theatre and seeing real actors treading the boards. I don't see the point, myself, actors can make mistakes when it's live, you can't guarantee the audience a perfect show. Not that Mr Griffin will even do rep work now; he doesn't like living in digs while a show's running. Mr Griffin basically doesn't like anything that involves leaving home these days. He sometimes gets work as a primary image, having graphic simulation computers scan his expression and vocal intonation so they can use it on the phaces they generate in the Web. That's drying up now; there's very little in the way of characteristics they can't emulate.

'Not to worry,' he said cheerfully. 'You're dressed up most splendidly today, young Aynsley. Going anywhere special?'

'Just the marshes. Thought I'd take a look, see if any new birds have got past the wardens.'

'Jolly good. Well, make sure you *stick to the path*.' He chuckled heavily, and gave me the kind of expectant expression that meant I was supposed to finish the joke.

I smiled awkwardly.

'Ah, well.' he said. 'Another piece of our heritage walks off into the new neon sunset.' He waved his secateurs at the football game. 'Did that lot give you any trouble today?'

'No.'

'Ha! Well, if they do, you remember to come and see me. I did my fair share of hell-raising when I was younger. Might look ancient, but I can still give those awful louts a shock.' He patted the slim black gadget clipped to his belt and winked.

I know what it is, because he told me. A sonic jet. They send out a vicious beam of noise that is intended to frighten the living daylights out of dogs. They work pretty well against muggers, too. The EU parliament hasn't outlawed them yet, but it's only a matter of time.

'I'll remember, Mr Griffin,' I promised.

There's no clear cut boundary where the field ends and the nature reserve begins. The grass just gradually gets longer and reedier, the soil becomes softer. I kept to the dirt track that the wardens drive their Land-Rovers along. It's a public bridle path on the map.

After a couple of hundred metres the silence closed in, wrapping round me like a thick extra coat. I couldn't see the bungalows or the field any more. Puddles of stagnant, reddy-brown water were appearing on either side of the track. All the grass stems and reeds were sprinkled with grey droplets, as if colour was leaking out of the world.

Things were scurrying through the undergrowth on all sides of me. Small animals, voles and rabbits, I suppose. Not being able to see them made it creepy. I could hear them brushing through the reeds and making tiny splashes in the puddles.

Eventually, I came to the fence. I'd only ever been this far once before. That was a year ago when we had one of our rare family walks. It was a sturdy chain-link mesh, well over two metres high. One of the posts had a sign bolted to it, saying: RESTRICTED AREA. KEEP OUT. WETLAND

ENVIRONMENT RESTORATION WORK IN PRO-
GRESS. PUBLIC ADMISSION TO RECOMMENCE IN
JANUARY 2032. *This is an EU Environmental Initiative co-
funded by Bigene Industrie, Civil Development Division.*

I always got a strange feeling reading that name out here
in the middle of the remote wilderness. Fancy Bigene
Industrie at work just a few kilometres from my front door.
It's a huge Anglo-French biotechnology company, a world
leader. Politicians in Brussels are always holding it up as an
example of successful European collaboration. It supplied
the biological recycling system for the three-man Olympus
craft that uses genetically engineered microbes and algae to
clean and purify the air and water used by the crew. The
Mars mission is the first time biological recycling has been
employed during a manned spaceflight of such length.
Bigene also developed the jockey chip with which the
mission commander, Colonel McFarlane, is fitted. The
jockey chip reads his nerve impulses directly, a new concept
in providing a remote rider, which they hope will eliminate
the Websuit provider mode altogether. When he steps out
on to the planet's surface in two days time, everyone
wearing a Websuit in receiver mode will know exactly what
it's like, what he sees and feels setting foot on Mars.

The reason Bigene Industrie is working around The Wash
area is because of their energy division. They were heavily
involved with building the solar hydrogen stations. Out in
The Wash are huge (10 kilometres in diameter) circular
mats floating on the top of the sea. They're made out of
plastic like the sheets of bubble polythene that people use
to insulate their greenhouses in winter. Except, instead of
air in the bubbles, the mats contain a genetically engineered algae. When the sun shines the algae's photosynthe-
sis splits sea water up into hydrogen and oxygen. The gas
then gets pumped ashore to be burned in a power station.
And the wonderful thing about it is, burning hydrogen
means there is absolutely no pollution. The only waste
product is steam; which is cooled into fresh water to
complement the desalinization plants that are being built

all round the coastline to compensate for the reduced rainfall.

The Brussels Energy Directorate already wants to quadruple the number of mats in The Wash over the next ten years; and other European shallow-water basins are being investigated to see if they can be used to anchor mats as well. Some people worried about the damage such a huge project would cause to the coastline while the mat anchors were being installed, the hydrogen pipes laid, and the power station was built. That's why Bigene helped to restore the marshes, and all the other sections of wild coastline along The Wash, to prove there would be no longer term environmental damage. They actually improved the area beside Heacham; the marshes here were drying out and dying from the seven-month summers and tiny annual rainfall we get now. Bigene Industrie's crews completely transformed them, putting in new networks of channels and small dams to hold the water.

I looked through the fence. The marsh on the other side seemed exactly the same. But if the company experts said it wasn't settled yet, I could hardly argue.

Something dark darted about in the shadows behind a clump of reeds about twenty metres away on the other side of the fence. So fast it was almost impossible to tell if it was real or not. It must have been real, though, because I yelped in surprise. I thought— All right, I'll be honest. I thought it was a spider; one of the kind used in the Web to warn you off forbidden areas. Which is a real one-mip idea – that something from the Web could be wandering round a Realworld marsh.

I stared at the clump of reeds until my eyes grew tired and it was hard to focus. But nothing moved again. Being in the marsh spooked me, that's what it was. My imagination was getting all hyped up.

I sighed and set off along the fence towards where I thought I'd seen the lightstorms. Two minutes later, I found it!

CHAPTER THREE

HEADLONG INTO A
WALL OF STONE PIXELS

'What do you mean, burned?' Katie asked.

'Just that,' I told them. I flapped my bird-form wings for emphasis. 'The ground and the reeds were all burned, completely roasted. It was a patch about three metres wide. Even the fence chain was black with soot.

'Told you!' Selim said triumphantly. 'It's the exhaust jet from a flying saucer.'

'A very small saucer, if its engine exhaust only burned a circle three metres wide,' Bayliss said.

'They are supposed to be *little* green men,' I said.

'We all laughed at that, except for Selim.

'Ha ha,' he grunted. 'So what do you think it is then, million-mip brains?'

'I'm not sure,' Bayliss said. 'The light Aynsley sees is obviously some kind of flame to have produced the scorch effect he found. But my knowbot couldn't find any explanation other than will-o'-the-wisps.'

'Mine too,' Katie admitted.

Selim and Drunlo confessed to similar results.

'Could it be local kids sneaking in there to let off fireworks?' Bayliss asked. 'Guy Fawkes night was only a week ago, after all.'

'What night?' Drunlo asked.

'Guy Fawkes,' I said. 'It's a celebration when the English let off fireworks; like the fourth of July for Americans and Bastille Day in France. Why, don't you have any national days like that?'

'Not really.'

I didn't press. You don't, not in the Web. Your friends tell you all they want to about themselves, nothing more. I realized I didn't even know what nationality Drunlo was. It doesn't matter. He was good company, a competent gamer. Who needs more from people?

'So, is it fireworks?' Selim asked.

'I really don't think so. The marsh is pretty remote from the rest of the village. And you have to walk past a whole row of bungalows to get to it. If people had been doing that it would be noticed, even at night. Several of my neighbours have got dogs.'

'All right, we know the lightstorms are definitely real,' Bayliss said. 'Can anyone think of a natural explanation?'

None of us could.

'Then you have to report it,' he said.

I just knew he was going to say that. 'Do I have to?' I moaned. I try and live as quietly as I can; kicking up a fuss about weird fires was going to draw attention to me no matter what the outcome.

'Something dangerous and quite possibly illegal is going on in your community,' Bayliss said, he sounded quite offended. 'It's your duty as a citizen to inform the authorities.'

'OK, I suppose so.'

'We'll spin in with you,' Katie said. Her Rebecca Ryan smile of reassurance was captivating.

'Hey, if there's a reward, do we share it?' Selim asked.

'Oh, curl up!'

Community policing is a major Federal policy. Actually, anything with 'community' in the title is a major part of Federal policy. The theory is that having regular, concerned, helpful police officers patrolling your neighbourhood twenty-four hours a day should inspire people's confidence in the forces of law and order and deter the local criminal element. Unfortunately, Realworld policies like that cost an awful lot of money to maintain. So, regional police forces moved into the Web big-time.

Heacham police station was actually a reception and filter subsection in the King's Lynn police site. Someone had the bright idea of making it one of these old-fashioned village policeman's houses with a one room station on the ground floor. Just to make sure the cliché was completely vom inducing, its phace was a wise-old-man desk sergeant in a 1950s uniform (pointed hat, whistle on a chain, and everything!). I wouldn't mind, but the police obviously weren't allocating much capacity to the program; there was too much green everywhere, the structure had translucent speckles running through it, and the phace sergeant's lip movement weren't quite in sync with his voice.

'Now then, youngsters,' he said. 'What can I do for you, then?'

I didn't dare risk a glance at the others. 'I've seen some lights,' I said. 'Out over the marsh at night.'

'Have you now? Well, there's a thing and no mistake. You were quite right to bring it to my attention, master Aynsley. You never know what kind of villainous business is afoot, even in a village as quite as our—' the whole site flickered, buzzing loudly, as the standard program shunted in its user designation '—Heacham. We always rely on the public to keep their eyes peeled to help prevent wrong-doing.' He flipped open a small black leather notebook and licked the tip of his pencil. (No, look, I'm not making this up, honest!) 'Now then, why don't you give me a properly detailed description of the incident? After that, I can decide what action will be appropriate.'

I *really* wished we hadn't spun in. But I told him anyway, then waited while the phace sergeant froze and the site flickered and buzzed some more. Eventually, the program ran my story through all its analysis levels and produced the relevant response.

'Well now, youngsters, I want you to know you have done entirely the right thing in coming to the police with this. Fortunately, you have nothing to worry about. Lights that appear over marshy areas are called will-o'-the-wisps.'

'We *know*—' Bayliss began in exasperation.

'They are completely natural and harmless,' the sergeant continued impassively. 'If you require more information to reassure yourselves, please access an educational site and ask for the appropriate file.'

'You mean you're not going to do anything?' Katie asked.

'There is no need to inform my superiors. Thank you for coming to see me. And if you see anything unusual in future, please don't hesitate to report it.'

'Does a landing by the scout force of an alien invasion fleet count as unusual?' Selim grumbled.

The site flickered alarmingly as the program started to process what he said.

'Come on,' I said. We spun out.

'I have never accessed such a worthless program,' Bayliss protested. 'Never! We have a legitimate cause for concern, and it won't even advance us to a genuine detective. What kind of law and order do you have in your country, Aynsley?'

'Good, usually,' I said meekly. 'The police are rather short of money, as always. They can't upgrade every program. If I'd seen a murder the phace would have brought a real detective on line for us.'

'Perhaps we should tell it that,' Drunlo said. 'Then you could explain to the detective what the real problem is.'

'Er ... I think there are some rather stiff penalties for supplying false data to police programs. Lots worse than getting spidered off.'

'So, now what?' Katie asked.

'Aynsley could always phone the police station in King's Lynn directly and try and talk to a real officer,' Selim suggested.

'The phone computer has a reception and filter program, too,' I said. 'It's even less sophisticated than the Heacham site.'

'There is one other approach we could try,' Bayliss said. 'Contact someone who's far more concerned about the marsh and what's happening to it than the police.'

The bat lasted longer than normal when I spun into Bigene Industrie's site. They didn't want to let my avatar in. They had a human-form only law which was even stricter than Tropicana's, but my Equal Access Program overrode it.

We emerged on a small grassy park that surrounded a fifty-storey skyscraper built out of silver glass and black marble. One of thousands of skyscrapers in a city that was a merger between real New York and a science fiction pulp magazine metropolis. I half expected to see atomic powered aircars whizzing about overhead, but the International Trade Block is too conservative for that. Each of those gleaming towers represents the sum total of a company's processing and memory capacity. The bigger the skyscraper the bigger the company. There weren't many taller than Bigene Industrie's.

The five of us went into the reception lobby. It looked like a cathedral inside; only instead of stained glass the arching windows were displaying company projects. I saw pictures of the Olympus mission, medical stuff, funny-looking plants, even a satellite's view of the mats in The Wash.

'Can I help you?' the receptionist asked with a friendly smile. This phace was generations of upgrades ahead of the police sergeant. He was laughable, she was a bit . . . intimidating, I suppose. She outshone Rebecca Ryan effort-lessly in the beauty stakes, and she was wearing this autumn's Paris fashions.

'I'd like to report some fires,' I said.

Something really odd happened while I blundered through my explanation. The phace got better. All right, I'm not a Web graphics expert, but I've been in enough sites in my time to know the score. The gamer and leisure companies go all out to perfect realism, they have to if they want to attract people into their sites. Other than that, sites use commercially available cog image generating programs. Their quality depends on how much processing capacity the operator wants to spend their money on; or, in the case of police and other civil service departments, how much they've been budgeted.

By the time I'd finished describing the lightstorms, the receptionist was more substantial than half the Realworld people I know. Luscious thick hair with every strand groomed into place, every crease and fold on her suit crisply defined, and rustling as she moved. There were even pores on her skin. I saw a ring on her left index finger, a big red stone on a plain gold band. I couldn't remember that being there when we spun in.

'There's nothing to worry about,' she said sweetly. Even her voice was different, becoming very authoritative, yet at the same time reassuring. 'Wild fires are nature's way of restoring the land, and regenerating the local ecology.'

'There were dead birds,' I told her. 'I saw them. They'd been caught in the flame. That whole marsh is a nature reserve, there must be thousands of birds and animals sheltering there. If these wild fires keep happening won't they be in danger?'

'With this year's low rainfall, I'm afraid such outbreaks are inevitable. It might seem a harsh method of clearing dead vegetation, but it is actually good for the marsh in the long run. If you examine the scorched areas in the spring you will find them thriving with new and vigorous shoots. Ultimately, that increases the food supply for local wildlife, allowing the marsh to sustain an even larger number of animals and birds.'

'Oh.'

'Rest assured, our teams will already be monitoring the situation. If the outbreak of wild fires ever appears to be presenting any kind of hazard then steps will be taken. However, as we're now well into autumn, it's safe to say that the worst is already over. If you would like, I can provide you with a Bigene Industrie ecology information pack. It would give you a better understanding of how regenerated habitats are managed. Our experience is unrivalled in this area. The Wash coastline is only one of our successes. We are involved in many regional improvement schemes all over the world.'

'That's very kind,' Bayliss said quickly. 'But we just wanted to make sure that there wasn't anything wrong with the marsh.'

'I hope I have been of some assistance.'

'You have,' he said brightly. 'Come on guys, time we spun out.'

'So what do you think?' Katie asked when we spun back to the Tropicana.

'I think we're on to something,' Bayliss said.

'You saw the way the receptionist phace changed?' I enquired.

'I saw it. Bigene Industrie must have tripled the processing power they were using to generate her.'

'But why?' Drunlo asked.

'To make her convincing,' I said. 'And I don't just mean making sure we couldn't see the gaps between her pixels. She was way too silky; we were being spidered off. They wanted that explanation to convince us. All that bitslag about outbreaks of wild fire being perfectly natural. What do they think we are? One-mips!'

'They were definitely trying to bluff us over the light-storms,' Bayliss said. 'But that still doesn't tell us what's causing them, nor what they actually are.'

'Perhaps if we went back to the police,' Katie said. 'Tell them that the company is hiding something out there.'

We can't prove it, though,' Selim said. 'We all know that they upgraded the phace, and why, but that's hardly evidence.'

'How can we force them to admit it?' Katie asked. 'Could we go to an environmental group like Greenpeace?'

'They'll say the same thing as the police,' Bayliss said. 'We don't have any evidence. And they can't go around spamming the Web with allegations about Bigene Industrie. We need a lot more information.'

'What about a court case?' Drunlo asked. 'Force the company to hand over its files on the marsh to us.'

'Do you have the money for that?' Katie asked. 'I certainly don't. In any case, it would take ten years.'

'There may be a way to get the right information out of Bigene Industrie,' I said.

'*How?*' they chorused.

'I don't know about the actual method. But I know someone who does.' It was time to pay Uncle Elton a visit. One of him, anyway.

CHAPTER FOUR

A TRIP TO THE LIBRARY

I wasn't supposed to be doing this. Heavens, I'm not even supposed to know about it.

Dad was in his office, busy saving industry from government. Mum wasn't back. Edwyn was wearing his gag.

I sneaked into the kitchen, which Mum uses as her cocoon. Her computer tower was standing at the end of the worktop, along with a laser printer, gag set, keyboard, and 3-D screen. I switched it on and plugged my Websuit in.

The bat left me standing on a giant chessboard of blue and green squares two metres across. Translucent pink cubes, a metre high, were sitting on some of the squares. The whole arrangement resembled a miniature, and very crude, version of Webtown's first level. Each of the cubes was a file in the computer's memory, names and numbers floated inside them like tiny neon signs.

'Uncle Elton?' I called. 'It's me, Aynsley.'

He popped up from behind one of the cubes, looking round furtively. 'Aynsley, nice to see you, lad. Humm. It's been fifty days since your last visit.'

'I didn't know I was supposed to come more regularly.'

'You're not. We're all free agents.'

'Right.' I think Uncle Elton had absorbed a lot more of Grandpa's ideology than Mum ever did.

He sat on one of the cubes and took up the classic 'thinker' pose, one fist tucked under his chin. 'Sit down, lad. How's things outside? Those kids from the other bungalows still giving you a hard time?'

He's a phace, of course, a very good one. The police came

to our house when he (the real Uncle Elton, that is) was arrested, searching for his memory files. They didn't find any. I still don't know how he and Mum hid them from police knowbots; my computer memory was nearly scrambled after they'd spun in and browsed. I never realized how strong sibling loyalty could get; I doubt I'd ever do Edwyn a favour like this, and I *know* he wouldn't do it for me.

I glided over to Uncle Elton and perched on the next cube. 'It's not so bad at the moment.'

'Ah, that's the bonus of growing old. Some things get easier, while life itself becomes more complicated.'

'I've got a problem, Uncle Elton. I need someone who knows a lot about the Web to help me.'

'Aynsley, I love you dearly; but your mother would wipe every megabyte of me from her tower if I got you involved in anything disreputable.'

'Too late for that. There's a company that my friends and I think is trying to cover up something funny out in the marsh. I need to know how to get into its files.'

'A corporate conspiracy, you say? How intriguing. I thought mad billionaires trying to take over the world ended when they stopped making James Bond films. Tell me more.'

'Why are we here?' Katie asked after we spun in.

I glanced round. The British Library site had the same kind of dimensions as a cathedral. Its walls were made up from bookshelves of ancient, polished oak; with seven wide balconies on each side running down the entire length. There must have been millions of books up there, everything from national records to current fiction; the library had an on-line copy of almost anything published in England during the last five centuries. A regiment of reading tables took up most of the central aisle; with people studying huge tomes, their faces illuminated by images scurrying across the paper. A crisscross of delicate bridges spanned the gap overhead, linking together the various balconies.

'Because it's old, Katie. The library has been on-line for decades in various forms; it's had hundreds of upgrades and augmentations. They just keep adding and adding to it, and now nobody quite knows what's in it any more. Uncle Elton says there are chunks of hardware that date back to the early nineties still operating here.'

'How does that help us?' Selim asked.

'It's got a vast amount of memory which is hardly ever accessed, and certainly never checked. That means it acts like a magnet for certain things.'

'Such as?'

'Programs that Uncle Elton says can be useful to us. Now, I want you all to split up and start browsing the book-shelves. I don't want a file, you're looking for holes in the shelving fabric itself. As soon as you find one, let me know.'

'What sort of holes?'

'One that doesn't belong. It'll look like it's been chewed out, OK?'

They all drifted away from me, except for Drunlo.

'You're trying to find a cyberat, aren't you?' he demanded. His voice and expression showed how unhappy he was with the idea.

'That's right. I need one.'

Cyberats are old viruses that have *evolved* in the Web. The experts, programmers and lawyers, haven't made up their minds whether they're alive, but they're certainly self-governing, and smart in their own way. They hunt down sections of spare memory where they can live/store them-selves without whoever owns the hardware knowing about it. There was even a case earlier in the year when some kind of viruses interfaced with phaces in the GulliverZone to produce self-aware programs, what people called digital life. The UN Court of Human Rights wound up granting them citizenship. Cyberats don't have quite that mips level, but their access and integration ability is formidable. Once one of them gets into your processor it's very difficult to wipe it.

'What are you going to do with it?' Drunlo asked.

'I want to store it in a hardblock memory, then take it to another site.'

'Are you going to try and alter its format?'

'No. I don't know how to, anyway.'

'All right,' he said, with obvious reluctance. 'I'll help you.'

'Thanks.' I didn't quite understand what the problem was. But he would help. Drunlo is very blunt in some things. I think he's one of the most honest people I've ever met. I suppose that's why I like him.

Bayliss found the hole. We gathered round the shelf on the third balcony where the wooden surface had a chunk missing. It was on the upright section at the end of the shelf, just beside the eight volumes of Neil Kinnock's biography. A circle of wood ten centimetres across simply didn't exist any more, there was only an infinite black cavity.

'Where does it go?' Selim asked.

I tapped the thick leather-bound books. 'Probably into their storage space. The cyberat should be safe in there; this hole is just its access portal.'

'A cyberat! Is this a bad bite, Aynsley?'

'No, sorry. This is for real.'

'But they're dangerous. It could get back into our computers, we'd lose everything.'

'That's a myth. Cyberats aren't interested in home systems; we power down too often. They want permanent on-line sites. That's why they move around so much, so they don't get trapped by a systems check.'

He grunted. Obviously not convinced.

'Keep watching,' I told them. 'Make sure no one is looking at us.' I closed my eyes, cutting myself off from the sight of the library. That made it easier for me to concentrate on the Websuit's keyboard. I tapped in the function I wanted. It had taken me over two hours to assemble the hardblock stack and interface it with my tower the way Uncle Elton had told me.

When I opened my eyes, I was holding a small cube in

the claws on the end of my wing. It glowed a radioactive blue. If I looked closely at it, I could make out narrow black grid lines just under the surface, they curved back towards the centre, forming a funnel that stretched backwards for ever. Every surface had the same effect; it was as though the inside of the cube contained an entire universe.

I put it on the bookshelf, right up against the hole.

'What is that thing?' Bayliss asked.

'A rat trap. To the cyberat, it'll seem as though the cube contains a huge empty storage space. It won't be able to resist that. Then when it goes in—'

'Snap!' Katie said loudly. She brought her hands together, and grinned. 'We got it.'

'That's right.'

'What exactly does this uncle of yours do?' Bayliss asked. 'I wouldn't know how to put together a storage space trick like that.'

'He was a consultant for a multimedia company.'

'Was?'

'He took early retirement.' One thing Websuits can't do even on realoe mode is replicate the way your skin changes colour when it heats up. I was mighty glad about that. I could feel a heavy blush rising up my cheeks.

'There!' Katie squealed, pointing excitedly.

I glanced over at the shelf. Even on Webtime, I was almost not quick enough.

The cyberat darted across the gap between its portal hole and the glowing blue cube. According to Web-myth, there are hundreds of different types. They don't breed, exactly, although they constantly duplicate themselves; but they do exchange sub-routines to keep mutating and stay one step ahead of systems check programs.

This one looked as though an ordinary rat had been remodelled by an aerospace design team, turning it missile-sleek and silver grey. The thing was amazingly *fast*.

A miniature portcullis slammed down across the cube's surface, then it turned green and let out a contented bleep. I picked it up. 'Time to visit Bigene Industrie again.'

CHAPTER FIVE

WHO SAYS SPIDERS
CAN'T FLY?

The spotless Bigene Industrie building loomed up in front
of us like some giant shiny gravestone. Possibly mine, if
things went down the plug.

'You sure about this?' Selim asked nervously.

Funny the one with doubts should be him, the most
headstrong of all of us.

'Not really,' I said. 'But I'm going to give it a go.'

'Good luck,' Katie said. She rubbed the top of my head;
which I suppose was the equivalent of a hug.

'You all know what to do?'

'Yes,' they chorused.

'We'll each start asking the receptionist phace for information,' Bayliss recited, determined to get it right. 'We can
say that it's research for school projects; companies are
always silky about public relations so the site will be
programmed to help as much as it can. It won't tie up
much processing capacity, but every little helps.'

'Too right,' I agreed. I spread my wings wide and
launched myself into the sky. When I looked down I could
see the others hurrying to the skyscraper's entrance. Large
blue-grey spiders were creeping in over the edge of the
small park, heading for the spot where we'd spun in. They
must have detected a program format violation when I took
off. I watched them converge then start circling round
looking for the guilty party. Bayliss and the others vanished
into the building. I raised my head and flapped upwards
enthusiastically.

It took me about a minute to reach the roof. By that time

the spiders down on the park were so small I could barely see them. The roof was just a blank ochre rectangle, without a single feature. I landed in the middle, and glanced round cautiously. No spiders in sight up here.

'The one thing you must not allow to happen,' Uncle Elton had warned me sternly, 'is to let a spider touch you. The Web allows every user complete anonymity, and ordinarily you cannot be traced. But if one of Bigene Industrie's guardian spiders attaches itself to you, they'll be able to check out where the avatar is interfacing with the Web. They'll know who you are, and probably a lot more than that. You wouldn't believe how much personal information is stored in memory banks these days.'

I held out the green rat trap in my left claw, and used my right hand to tap out the release code on my Websuit pad. The cube's surfaces flashed blue for a second, and the cyberat shot out. It crouched on the roof, giving me a terrible stare with glinting scarlet eyes, then it was running backwards and forwards, its nose pressed against the smooth ochre.

The wretched thing must have taken about ninety seconds to find a weak spot in the site's texture. It felt like ninety hours. Uncle Elton told me cyberats hated being exposed: the first thing it would do after it was released was find a part of the site program where it could conceal itself. It stopped abruptly, and virtually head-butted the roof. I couldn't see any difference between the part it had chosen and any other. Jaws like small JCB scoop clamps began to chew at the ochre surface.

I spread my wings wide, took a couple of paces, and launched myself, gliding slowly towards the cyberat as it disappeared down the hole it was gnawing. My fingers tapping furiously on the Websuit pad, changing the avatar's scale. Another appalling breach of Web etiquette. I shrunk as I flew, which made the distance to the cyberat's hole grow larger and larger the whole time. I've never come so close to the voms before, swooping forward at the same time I was receding. Confusing, or what? The whole site world was getting bigger; the rooftop was at least the size of a continent. When the alteration finished I was actually smaller then the cyberat. The hole was like an empty black crater ahead of me. I didn't like to think what the cyberat would do to my diminished Websuit programs if we bumped into each other now. Uncle Elton had just shrugged rather apologetically when I asked him.

Something moved out by the edge of the roof. An Everest-size volcano erupting up over the horizon. Then another one appeared, bending in the middle. Spider legs! Titan-sized spider legs. It must have climbed up the side of the skyscraper. Two more groped their way over the edge, and all four tensed, starting to lever the body up. It would be as big as a moon!

I didn't wait to check. Head to head with the cyberat would be like meeting an angel compared to that. I dived down into the hole.

Another city of skyscrapers waited for me inside. I plummeted out of a tiny black gap in the solid sky, tumbling completely out of control. It took me ages to steady myself, twisting my wing tips to oppose the spin, slowing and levelling out. I was already perilously close to the tops of the skyscrapers before I was flying horizontally again. But I was in! I could hardly believe I'd done it. Uncle Elton was a genius.

I tapped out the code to expand my avatar scale again. This city was different to the one outside. For a start, I could see the walls, cold steel-grey squares stacked like bricks. The odd thing was, the space inside the Bigene Industrie building was much bigger than it appeared from outside. Or maybe I just hadn't got the scale right. The other thing was, the skyscrapers inside weren't skyscapers at all; they were old-fashioned metal filing cabinets. Twenty-four of them. Each one had a white letter on the roof.

'Just pray,' Uncle Elton had told me, 'that they use ordinary names to label their files.'

I was gliding over T, heading towards S. What I wanted was H, for Heacham.

'Or maybe W for The Wash,' Uncle Elton had mused.
'Perhaps M for marsh. Then again, it could even be under R
for reclamation, and you'll have to start cross referencing.'

I banked steeply, almost tilting my outstretched wings to
the vertical, and turned hard around R before righting
myself. H was dead ahead now, three cabinets away.

Spiders were running along the road below. Dozens of
them, easily my size, with green and yellow skin patterned
the same as a tiger.

So far, none of them were looking up, but it would only
be a matter of time. I needed a diversion, and fast. H was
one cabinet in front now. I turned quickly, swooping round
M and heading for N. The rat trap was still held in my left
claw. It flashed blue as I tapped in the release code again. A
cyberat dropped out, and plummeted down on to the road.

You see, the hardblock contained a permanent record of
the cyberat; it could churn out as many copies as I wanted. I
flew between the cabinets, dropping cyberats as I went, the
rat trap cube strobing like some kind of police-car light.
They landed on the road and immediately raced for the
base of the nearest cabinet, sensing the colossal amount of
memory contained inside. I must have let thirty or forty fall
before I turned back.

The spiders went berserk. They came charging down
every road towards the cyberats, chasing them round the
cabinets in dizzy circles. One on one, they were evenly
matched, producing a fight which was gory without any
actual blood. The spiders tried to gobble up the cyberats;
while the cyberats bit off spider legs with their spring-trap
jaws. I saw several spiders reduced to immobile bodies with
heads flexing round helplessly. After a while, such casualties would simply fade out of existence. New spiders were
still running in towards the conflict, outnumbering the
cyberats quite heavily now. They were going to win
eventually.

I reached the H filing cabinet. There were no spiders
anywhere near its base. The front of the filing cabinet was
made up of drawers, fifteen of them. They were all labelled,

starting with Ha-Hc on the top, then Hd-Hf, and so on down to the ground. The top corner of each one had a small nine pad keyboard.

Theoretically, anything to do with Heacham should have been in the second drawer, Hd-Hf. I glided in as near as I could to take a closer look. The keyboard protruded from the drawer by about twenty-five centimetres. Just big enough. I spiralled round and made another pass. This time I held out the rat trap and entered the release code. A cyberat popped out on to the narrow ledge formed by the top of the keyboard. It gave me its usual red-eyed glare, then looked from side to side. I suppose it must have known how close to the memory space it was, and the only thing blocking it from access was the entry code. I watched as it stretched itself tentatively over the edge of the ledge to study the keyboard pads.

That was when I saw a spider creeping its way up the cabinet, its legs moving in purposeful judders. I dived down the front of the drawers, heading for the spider like a jet fighter. It stopped its climb, the front two legs waggling in agitation. The rat trap was disgorging a torrent of cyberats which fell straight towards it. Five of them thumped straight into it. They immediately started snapping and chewing at its striped flanks. It lost its grip, and they all crashed down on to the road together.

Three more spiders had arrived by the time it hit. Two of them began chasing the sinuous cyberats as they sprinted for cover, while the third stayed put, watching me. I didn't like that at all. They'd obviously worked out that I was the cause of all the trouble.

I began a complete circuit of the cabinet. The spider scurried along underneath me, matching my movements perfectly. Cyberats were falling like rain all around it, but it never diverged a centimeter. Of course, as it didn't threaten them, they ignored it.

There was a full scale battle between cyberats and spiders going on by the time I got back to the front of the cabinet. This time the cyberats were in serious trouble; their jaws no longer had any effect against the spiders. No matter how fast or agile they were, they couldn't avoid the even faster mandibles that snatched them up, drew them backwards into gaping empty mouths and swallowed them up.

The spiders had learned and adapted. I was getting a real bad feeling about this. The only advantage I had left now was speed. My thumb located the Websuit's scuttle button, and rested on it lightly. Just in case.

I pumped my wings hard, desperate for altitude and as much distance from that horribly knowledgeable spider as I could get. Up above me, I could see the cyberat I'd left on the keyboard. It was hanging dangerously over the edge, using its forepaws to tap in a code on the numbered pads. Drawer Hd-Hf began to slide out from the cabinet. I'd done it! That spider would never climb all the way up here in time.

I soared up over the top of the open drawer just as the cyerat dived inside. It was full of slim folders packed together tight enough to form a solid floor, there must have been a thousand of them. They began to ripple slightly, like the surface of a lake with a big fish swimming just underneath. The ripples began to fan out, producing a V-shaped wake. It must have been the cyberat moving through them, heading deeper into the cabinet.

I glanced down to check on the spider that had been following me. That was when I saw *it*. A spider floating in the air between the cabinets, heading straight for me! Impossible. Then I glimpsed a tiny line of shimmering silver light stretching out from its abdomen right away up towards the roof. It was gossamer riding. Spiders do that in Realworld, hanging on to long lengths of their own thread, and letting the wind take them wherever it blows. If a thermal takes them high enough they can sometimes drift across seas.

It would get to the drawer long before I'd have a chance to find the Heacham file. I had no doubt it would be one of the new ones, immune to a cyberat. The scuttle button seemed to itch against my thumb.

I'd come so far, it didn't seem fair to lose now. Uncle Elton wouldn't be defeated by the brute, I was sure of that. He'd find a weakness to exploit. Pity I wasn't Uncle Elton.

I studied it again, desperate for some sign of vulnerability. My only weapon was the cyberat, and that wasn't any good against the spiders any more. So – I yelped in delight and launched myself straight towards it. The spider kept coming, imperturbably; its legs flexed eagerly, as if it were beckoning to me. I pitched up sharply, zooming for the sky. The gossamer strand was rushing past my nose. I was ten metres above the spider when I pivoted over, twisting through ninety degrees. As soon as I was at the top of the arc, I pressed the release code, and a cyberat was expelled from the rat trap.

All that time spent in combat sites had obviously paid off as far as my reflexes were concerned. OK, maybe there was some luck involved, too. But the cyberat shot straight into the gossamer. I held my breath.

The cyberat clung to the slender strand. For once it didn't glare at me. Too surprised at where it was, I expect. Its head came forward, metallic nose sniffing at the gossamer, then it bit through cleanly. The spider hurtled straight down.

I turned again and sped back to the open drawer. There was no mysterious wake left on the folders, no sign of the cyberat. I landed on the first file and ran forwards. Names skidded past under my clawed feet.

HEACHAM

I halted and went back a couple of paces. The top of the folder was about as wide as a floorboard. There were various symbols on either side of the name. I pressed *enter*, a circle with a vertical line bisecting it. The folder began to rise up. It was as if an ancient 2-D cinema screen was unfurling in front of me, and I had the only seat in the house.

I typed in the record code on my Websuit keyboard. The folder stopped rising when it was eight metres high. Text and wavy lines began to scroll down it.

Out of the corner of my eye I saw five more gossamer riding spiders sweeping towards the drawer. I stayed where I was for as long as I dared, watching the contents of the Heacham folder roll past in front of me. Then the spiders landed on the drawer. They darted forward, legs moving so fast they were a blur.

I pressed the scuttle.

The bat was sharp and nasty, too much like the unwanted jolt on a fairground ride that's gone wrong when you're at the highest point. I tried to calm my breathing when all the collapsing images stabilized into the neutral grey of an inactive Websuit visor.

My mind should have been bubbling over with elation. Instead, all I could feel was an awful depression. I'd read the text in the Heacham file as it scrolled past; or tried to. It wasn't in English. It wasn't in any language at all. It was just letters jumbled together at random. Utter rubbish.

CHAPTER SIX

THE PLOT THINS

'Of course it's rubbish,' Uncle Elton said in that scathing tone reserved for people who have been particularly daft. 'Everyone knows how easy it is to break into files these days.'

'*Easy*?'

'You did it and you're only ... er, how old are you now?'

'Mid-teens.'

'Exactly my point, lad. Mid-teens, and never spun an illegal bite in your life before; yet you waltzed straight in and helped yourself.'

'It wasn't quite a waltz, Uncle Elton.'

'Whatever. Security around the files is only the first line of defence, it can't be too strict because the company's own staff have to be able to access their data constantly. Think what Bigene Industrie keeps in those cabinets. All its finances, new bugs they've developed and haven't grown commercially yet, research data, marketing strategies, not to mention all the dubious goings on in the marshes. All immensely valuable in the wrong hands, which is very definitely you and I. So they simply encrypt the information they store.'

'Oh.' It made me feel a little better. Not much. Encryption was pretty obvious when you think about it.

'Let me have a look at what you got,' he said.

We were sitting on the pink cubes in Mum's computer again. I keyed in the recording I'd made, and the Heacham file appeared inside a d-box which hung in midair in front of us.

'All right, Aynsley, this is where it starts to get tricky.'

'Can you decrypt it for me?'

'Do cows leave pats behind them? I have a few tricks of the trade stored around here somewhere.' He walked over to one of the cubes and pulled a white cable from it with a complicated-looking socket on the end. The cable kept uncoiling behind him as he walked over to the d-box. He bent down and plugged the socket into the base of the d-box. 'Now, let's see how good I really am,' he said quietly.

Up on the screen, the jumbled letters were rearranging themselves into proper words. Wiggly lines straightened out into diagrams.

I start to read.

We found a table some distance from the others on the Tropicana beach. I set up a d-box on the sun-bleached wood, and keyed the code for Bigene Industrie's Heacham file. The d-box swam with colourful refraction patterns, then the text solidified. CLASSIFIED was printed boldly across the title page.

'What did we get?' Selim asked eagerly.

I could have said something about how it had suddenly become *we*. But Selim was Selim and, besides, having their complete support made me feel pretty good.

'The answer, I think,' I said.

'Great!'

'Tell us then. What are the lightstorms?' Bayliss asked.

I couldn't resist it. 'Will-o'-the-wisps.'

They all groaned.

'You're biting,' Katie exclaimed.

'No I'm not. It's just that these ones aren't exactly natural.' I scrolled the decrypted file until I came to the map of the marsh. It looked as if the land was coming out in a rash. Red blotches were dotted everywhere, some big, some small, there was no order to their size or location, it was completely random. The index called them *Dump Zones*.

'When the company was doing all that work reclaiming

the marsh, they built a lot of new water channels and ponds,' I said. 'They bulldozed a lot of soil about to make the banks, but they also brought in masses of landfill material as well. All perfectly legitimate, the EU Environmental officers approved the method. Some of the landfill was made up from old mats from The Wash. The EU people approved of that, too. The plastic is biodegradable, which means it can't spoil the earth it's buried in. The mats take quite a battering out on the sea and they have to be replaced every three or four years. The ones they used for the pilot scheme were starting to tear when the work on the marsh started, so everyone thought it would be a good thing to prove the old mats could be used beneficially. Bigene Industrie processed them with intense ultraviolet light to kill off the algae and make the plastic really brittle so it could decompose more easily. After that, the scraps were mixed with landfill and take out to the marsh.'

Bayliss clicked his fingers. 'They didn't process them,' he said.

'That's right. There was something in the file about the ultraviolet machine being delayed because of costs. So, rather than stall the whole project, they just mixed in the mats without treating them first. The algae was still alive when they buried it. And now the plastic is breaking down naturally, like it's supposed to, the algae is leaking out. Some of it is seeping into ponds, so when the sunlight shines, it's doing what it was designed to and splitting water into oxygen and hydrogen. Because it's such a light gas, most of the hydrogen disperses into the atmosphere, but quite a lot saturates the plants and dead vegetation. It's terribly volatile, the tiniest spark or static charge will ignite it. That's what I've been seeing, the hydrogen flaring off at night.'

'Aynsley, that is disgraceful,' Katie said. 'What a filthy way for the company to behave.'

'I know.' That was the part which worried me the most. Bigene Industrie had supplied the life support systems to the Olympus craft. The safety issue aside, I didn't want

companies that cut corners and cheated to have any part of
the Mars mission. It was too *grand* for that. Grandpa always
said it was a complete waste of money. I didn't disagree
with him on many things (didn't dare), but I did on this
occasion. I think the Olympus mission is a truly noble
venture. Most countries in the world have contributed to it;
some more than others, naturally. But everyone's involved,
helping to challenge the high frontier. And it's only today
that it's so difficult and costs so much. In a hundred years
time it won't be, purely because of the pioneering we're
doing now. To me, that's wonderful. I know the world isn't
perfect, but Olympus shows people what we can achieve as
a race if we really try. It's not just the hardware, the ships
and the landing craft; the spirit behind the venture is
equally important.

Bigene Industrie tainted that spirit.

'Now we can go back to the police,' Drunlo said. 'We
have all the proof we need.'

'What do you mean?' Bayliss asked, he sounded surprised
and shocked.

'We know that Bigene Industrie has been trying to cover
up a criminal act.' Drunlo pointed at my display sheet with
the incriminating map. 'When we show that to the police,
that one-mip phace sergeant will have to bring real
detectives on-line.'

Bayliss put his head in his hands and moaned. 'Brilliant!
And exactly what are you going to say to the police when
they ask how we got the Heacham file from Bigene
Industrie?'

Drunlo opened his mouth, then closed it. He scratched
his forehead, tilting his brown felt cap to one side. 'I hadn't
thought of that,' he finally admitted.

'This can't be a problem,' Katie said. 'Come on, guys, we
face paradoxes and puzzles much worse than this in the
games. There's got to be a way round it. Think! What's our
objective?'

'To alert the police about Bigene Industrie, and have
them investigated properly,' I said. 'I also want the marsh

to be made safe. Heaven only knows how much algae is leaking into the water.'

'Fine. So we have to produce some kind of rock-solid evidence other than the Heacham file to take to the police. Any ideas?'

'It will have to be the algae itself,' Bayliss said. 'A video of you collecting the sample would be useful, too.'

'Now wait a minute—'

'We know exactly where it is,' Selim said. His finger came down on one of the map's larger red blobs. 'You just have to go out there, scoop it up, and come back. What's the problem?'

'The problem! For a start most of the dump zones are inside the central fenced-off section of the marsh. The biggest one outside was the one I found; and that's already flared. I doubt there'll be much algae left. The flame killed everything else.'

'Then you'll have to go through the fence. You said it was only a chain link. A pair of bolt cutters will solve that. It'll be a doddle compared to accessing the files.'

'Really? Do you see that blue line that follows the fence on the inside?'

'Yes.'

'Look it up in the index.'

They all leaned over the data sheet.

'Guard dog run,' Bayliss read out. 'Ah, yes. That could be awkward.'

'What kind of weapons have you got?' Selim asked.

'Weapons? This isn't a gamer site we're studying! I don't pick up laser pistols and a bazooka when I spin in. There aren't power packs and jeeps and medical supplies left along the path that I can help myself to. This is Realworld we're talking about, Selim.'

'Ever heard of a sonic jet?'

'Yes, my neighbour has—' I jammed my mouth shut. Too late!

'Next problem,' Selim hooted.

'Simple,' I growled right back. 'We've just broken into

Bigene Industrie's files. They know someone's interested in the marsh. They'll be watching.'

'He's right,' Katie said.

'Then what we need is a time when they're not watching,' Bayliss said.

'It's their job, and they've been warned about a possible intrusion, they'll be watching the whole time.'

'Not necessarily. You're not taking human nature into consideration. What happens tomorrow night? November 15th, at twenty-one-hundred-hours to be precise.'

'The Mars landing.'

'Exactly. And everyone in the world who's on-line is going to spin in to the Olympus site so they can access Colonel McFarlane's jockey chip when he takes that step off the landing craft. The marsh security people included.'

'And me, too,' I said hotly. No way, absolutely no way on Earth was I going to miss the landing. Not me. I have lived and breathed the Olympus mission for the last three years.

'So give me another time,' Bayliss said.

Which must have been a rhetorical question, because anyone with his brains would know there wasn't an answer.

'In any case,' I said. 'That's in the middle of the night. I'm not creeping into the marshes by myself at night.'

'Of course not,' Katie said. 'We'll all be with you.'

'I don't think I can get all the way to England by then,' Drunlo said hastily.

She laughed. 'Not that way, not be there in Realworld. Aynsley can just switch his Websuit to provider mode.'

'Now just a—'

'Good idea,' Bayliss said. 'A portable terminal will be able to keep in touch with the low orbit communication satellite network the whole time. With them hooked in, they can triangulate your position and provide a navigation function. I've got the software in my portable if you haven't got a copy, Aynsley. You'll be able to walk straight to the dump zone with your eyes closed.'

'I'm not going.'

'What else is he going to need?' Selim asked
'I'm not going.'
They all stared at me.
'I'm not.'

CHAPTER SEVEN

THE MISSION PROFILE

Mars isn't a uniform all-over red like it appears from Earth. There are dark mountain ranges, plateaux, craters, polar caps, dry 'sea' beds. Hundreds of diverse, fascinating features. All visible with the naked eye from a thousand kilometre orbit.

I was looking down at the planet from the observation bubble in Olympus II, the *Eagle*. The other two Olympus ships were invisible, lost somewhere out among the empty blackness and strangely bright stars. In space, the stars don't twinkle. Only tens of kilometres of dusty, cloudy atmosphere makes them do that. Somehow, they look colder when they're burning steadily.

It's a weird sensation being completely passive, and yet feeling your body respond like a puppet to every move made by a total stranger. Receiver mode is one of the hardest Websuit functions to use. You have to really struggle against the urge to counter every motion, and just allow yourself to accept the ride you're getting.

That's what I did as I drifted forwards. My hand snatched up a carelessly discarded chocolate foil wrapper that was fluttering against the transparent bubble like a bizarre metallic bird. From my new position I could see along the side of the ship's cylindrical habitation module.

'Aynsley.'

The shell was a pale silver-white. A thick layer of thermal insulation foam coating the aluminium pressure vessel. Fifteen metres away, the landing craft was docked to the forward airlock.

'Aynsley, come on.'

It was a long aerodynamic cone with stubby triangular fins jutting out of the base, just above its heatshield. The landing pads were extended for testing, silvery insect-legs that seemed implausibly thin for the job they had to do. Somebody moved behind the tiny cockpit port.

'Aynsley, what are you doing in there?'

Mars quaked in front of me, its edges shivering.

I spun out back to my cocoon and flipped the Websuit visor up.

Mum was standing in front of me, her hand on my shoulder shaking me gently. Her face was full of sympathetic concern. 'Sorry, but you did say you wanted to go into King's Lynn this morning.'

'Yes, Mum.' I started to tug the suit off.

'What site were you in?'

'Olympus. They're going through the final checklists for the landing craft.' There is always one crew member in one of the three ships who is wearing a Websuit in provider mode. I've spun in more times than I can remember since they left Earth back in February. Freefall feels venomous, and on top of that I know exactly what it's like being a Realworld astronaut. No game.

'Aynsley, you will try and remember you have a life outside the Web.'

'Yes, Mum.'

She smiled softly. 'I know, I'm a sad old six cog.'

I do wish she wouldn't try to talk like that. 'You're not.'

'I know how wrapped up you are with the Mars landing, and I understand that, which is why I haven't objected yet.'

'To what?'

'The amount of time you spend accessing it. Mrs Lloyd spoke to me about it last week. Your grades are down, which is really unlike you. And she says you're becoming even more awkward at the physical fitness tutorials.'

'I'm not; I just think they're stupid, that's all.' Once a week I have to go into King's Lynn to be coached at dumb sports which I hate and am never going to be any good at.

It's the last remnant of the days when kids went to school in Realworld instead of using the Web to be educated like God intended. The government insists on keeping that aspect of the dark ages going, not just so we can all develop our talent to be Neanderthal football players or learn to be competitive (as if the Web games don't teach us that!) but so we can also develop our 'social interaction' skills. Social interaction, that is, with kids who have no common interest or even liking for each other, who treat anyone mildly different as an outcast, and take pleasure from doing so. You cannot find your peers out of a random selection of two hundred people; that only happens in the Web where like minds are drawn to the same sites. I rest my case.

'If you didn't take some exercise you'd inflate like a balloon, and be all podgy and horrible.'

'Who's going to care how I look in Realworld?'

I suppose it came out with more anger and bitterness than I mean. It certainly managed to hurt Mum, who sniffed hard and turned away to glance out of the window.

'I care,' she said quietly.

It must be awful for her to have a son she worries about the whole time, and who always says hurtful things to her. Maybe I don't think as fast as I claim I do, certainly not before I open my mouth.

'I know, Mum.' I smiled as an apology. She always says I never smile enough. 'I'll try not to be so awkward at the tutorials. But it's difficult with that Mrs Lloyd, you know? She's so ... enthusiastic.'

Mum laughed. 'Hard on skivers, you mean.'

Our car is a modified Mercedes EQ-250, an eight-seater that looks like a cross between a small freight van and a taxi. Mum waited until I was inside, then closed the rear door.

Apart for the trunk routes, most of the roads in England are starting to decay. County councils keep them clear enough for bike traffic, but that's about all. The Mercedes had broad, deep-tread tyres to cope with the grass and moss that was slowly spreading over the tarmac.

Several kids watched as we drove down the line of bungalows. I was pretty prominent sitting up in the back, looking down on them like royalty. For once there were no gestures, no taunts. Not with Mum driving. It was like divine protection.

'What do you want to buy?' she asked when we turned on to the A 149.

'Just some stuff for one of my projects.' It wasn't a lie, exactly. In fact, I wanted a special sensor and some new cards for a stack to augment my portable terminal ready for my trip into the marsh. But I could hardly tell her that.

The car's motorgas cell accelerated us silently up to seventy kilometres per hour. There were only a couple of delivery lorries on the road, and four or five bikes, their riders wrapped up against the chilly November air.

'Mum, what was Uncle Elton put in jail for?'

She didn't look round, but I could see her hands tighten on the wheel. 'What makes you ask that?'

'I was thinking about him. He doesn't seem like a criminal; he's the same as Grandpa really.'

'All right, I suppose you're old enough. But you must not tell Edwyn.'

'I promise.'

'Uncle Elton isn't a criminal. He just doesn't think, that's all. I blame Dad, your grandpa. Elton was a little too gullible for all that rebel philosophy Dad spouts. Don't you ever fall for any of it!'

'No, Mum, I won't.

'All right. Elton was listening to Dad rant on about the Establishment and how autocratic it is. He was young and hot-headed and decided that all that talk and moaning wasn't enough, he wanted to *do* something. Something which would knock the Brussels Parliament down a peg or two. Even I agreed with that; politicians are so pompous and stuffy. It doesn't hurt them to suffer a few indignities from time to time, show them that they aren't any better than the rest of us. As Elton worked for a multimedia company, it was easy enough. He set up a mock parliament site. Nothing illegal so far. But he went and loaded it into quite a few blocks he shouldn't have. I think the Tropicana was one of them. Even that wasn't so bad. His parliament's phace MPs were programmed to be satirical; they mocked and parodied everything their Realworld counterparts in Brussels said. But even that wasn't enough for Elton. Oh, no, he had them all sitting there stark naked.'

'*What*? All the MPs were nude?' I was giggling.

Mum was fighting a grin. 'Yes. He did exactly what he set out to do, and made them a laughing stock. His parliament was one of the most popular Web sites ever. Half of Europe spun in to see it. And when the real MPs started protesting about its existence, the phaces started complaining about *their* existence, claiming they were the true government. It all got quite surreal at the end.'

'And he got put in jail for that?'

'No. Not for satire. They got him on copyright violation. It's a famous law, at least to those of us who were in the media. Didn't you know, Aynsley, you own your own face. Nobody can reproduce your features without your permission. The law was intended to stop advertisers taking advantage of powerful simulation programs and duplicating a celebrity to endorse their products. But it applies to everyone. And Elton had replicated eight hundred MPs without their permission.'

'That's awful.'

'It's his own silly fault. The rule of law is paramount. If you break it, you are punished. That's a fundamental function of civilization; the law is there to protect us from other people behaving in a way that's likely to harm us. Some crimes are more serious than others, and there are degrees of criminal behaviour. Nothing in human behaviour is ever black and white, that's why we have the courts and judges, so they can determine exactly how bad the offence was and tailor the sentence to fit.'

'Do you think Uncle Elton should have been sent to jail?'

'Yes, but not for three years. Mind you, considering the people he annoyed, it was bound to happen.' She glanced at me in the rear-view mirror. 'Don't look so worried He's only in an open prison, not a maximum security one. The news sites are always complaining that they're more like holiday camps.'

'Good.' It wasn't Uncle Elton I was worried about, it was me! Breaking into Bigene Industrie's files meant I was already a criminal. Although they could never complain, because what they had done was far worse. I suppose that's what Mum meant about the courts establishing degrees of guilt.

We'd all just rushed headlong into this without thinking much about the rights and wrongs of what we were doing. And, to be honest, because it produced a thrill which no game ever did. But Realworld does have rules. What I had to start thinking about very seriously indeed was whether we were doing the right thing by breaking them.

Not that it was such a big offence. All I was doing was sneaking into the marsh to find some algae. Environmentalists had been doing that kind of thing for decades, forcing polluters to clean up their act. But did that make it right?

I pulled my mobile phone out and tapped in Katie's number. Out of all of us, she was the most level headed. I could confide my worry to her and get a sensible answer.

'Sorry, Aynsley,' Mum called out. 'Your call will have to wait. I've got to fill the tanks.'

We were turning into a garage. Its old petrol pumps were still in place, standing like rusty sentries underneath the broad canopy. I suppose it cost too much to dismantle them. There was no other reason for leaving them. England's last petrol-powered vehicle was withdrawn two years ago; I remember the ceremony on the news sites.

Mum drew up next to the motorgas terminus.

I frowned, not understanding why she'd told me to stop using the phone. Then I saw the warning sign next to the terminus, forbidding smoking, mobile phones, and telling drivers to switch off their collision alert radars. Motorgas was volatile stuff, it could be ignited easily.

I switched the mobile phone off, and stowed it back in my coat pocket. Perhaps it was for the best. What could I have said to Katie anyway?

I was committed to going into the marsh. Thinking about it, I had been right back from when I saw the first lightstorm.

CHAPTER EIGHT

THE NIGHT OF THE GREAT EXPEDITION

Colonel McFarlane gave the crew in the *Eagle* one last wave before closing the airlock hatch. He wriggled his way through the landing craft's cramped interior and settled into his pilot's seat. Two big holographic screens on his console were swirling with multicoloured graphics and flashing icons. Rows and rows of switches were illuminated with a faint blue glow.

'Stand by to initiate separation sequence,' he said.

That was when I spun out. I couldn't stand it any longer. If I'd kept watching for another minute I know I would have stayed in the GSA site until the landing and first footfall itself.

The only noise in my cocoon was the usual liquid gurgling from the central heating. All the stuff I'd need for the marsh was spread out waiting; clothes on the bed, electronics and hardware on the desk. It was eight thirty, and the night outside the window was a gloomy dark grey. I sighed, and started to get ready.

My clothes were the trickiest; I'd never even tried wearing a coat over the Websuit before. After a couple of minutes struggle I managed to wedge myself into it though it was an effort to move my arms. The first thing I noticed was how warm I'd become. I jammed the rest of my equipment into a shoulder bag, then plugged the Websuit into my portable terminal and checked the interface. Everything on-line.

I opened the door and peered out. There was no one around. I started down the corridor. Edwyn's door was closed. Mum and Dad were in the lounge, sitting on the settee. Both of them were in their Websuits. Their computer display showed me they were accessing the GSA's Olympus site for the landing. They would never even know I'd gone outside, let alone what I was doing there.

I hurried into the kitchen, then down the ramp. Fancy being in a hurry to do this! But in the house I was going from uncomfortably warm to sweltering. The night soon halted that. A sharp frost had settled, making every blade of grass shine a gritty white in the moonlight. Out over The Wash navigation lights were twinkling on the mat anchors, looking like a city skyline in the distance.

Once I was clear of the front garden I stopped and lowered my Websuit visor. I flicked the switch on the keyboard to *Provider*. Surprisingly, it didn't have cobwebs all over it. I can't remember the last time I used the suit in this mode, probably in the shop before I bought it. The night crept back in to surround me, exactly the same as before, relayed through the Websuit's vision sensor. All the suits come with a camera ring around the hood, like a small black crown. It gives the wearer, and anyone else accessing the output, a three-hundred and sixty degree field of vision. Having eyes in the back of your head is nothing compared to this. There's even a focus shift function so that you can move your viewpoint away from yourself. That was going to come in real handy tonight; when the others spun in they could keep watch all around me.

I brought two more programs on-line. The first was a light amplifier, which was like turning a huge floodlight on above the bungalows. It turned the world a weird green, but meant I could see everything almost as clearly as I could in the daytime. There was a cat slinking along Mr Griffin's rickety fence, a fat ginger one pausing every couple of paces to glance round furtively. I clapped my hands, and it looked up abruptly, moving its head from side to side to try to see where the noise came from. I clapped my hands again. The cat looked back the way it had come, completely perplexed. I could see it, but it couldn't see me!

The second program automatically elevated my view-point by fifty centimetres. When I looked down at my own body, I appeared to be wearing a thick green oilskin and slightly faded denim jeans; I had sturdy hiking boots on my feet, and woolly red socks that came up almost to my knees. This particular program was something else I hadn't used since I got the Websuit, I prefer the bird-form avatar.

With everything on-line, I hooked my portable terminal into the Web, creating my own private micro-site around me. Bayliss, Katie, Selim, and Drunlo spun in. The terminal assigned each of them a different viewpoint from the camera ring, and their familiar avatars materialized. It appeared as if they were standing right beside me.

They looked round slowly, taking it all in.

'Are those the mats?' Katie asked, pointing at the constellation of lights gleaming offshore.

'That's their anchors you're seeing, yes. They're like iron pillars that are sunk real deep into the sand so they stay put. There's six of them for each mat, one at each corner.'

'And you live here, in this?' Drunlo asked. He was staring at the boat with his hands on his hips and his head cocked to one side.

'Yep.'

'That's *strange*, Aynsley.'

'Not really. Mum always says she's waiting for a really high tide, so we'll be swept out to sea. That way life will be more interesting, never knowing which country you're going to wash up on.'

His expression told me he thought that was even stranger than the house itself.

'Then this must be the marsh,' Bayliss said. He had walked a few paces away to stand on the track so he could face the darkest section of the horizon.

'That's right.'

'Come on then,' Selim said eagerly. 'What are we waiting for?'

I started off down the track. I checked once, just to see if the program was holding up. My boots were crunching through the frosty grass, even leaving footprints behind.

'Did you manage to get all the equipment we talked about?' Bayliss asked.

'Sure. But if that sonic jet doesn't work, then we're calling the whole thing off.'

'Of course.'

The marsh at night looked completely different. I could see the path easily enough, but the light amplifier changed the long grass and reeds to peculiar white fronds dancing about in the breeze. The navigation program was up and running in a d-box, showing me exactly where I was on the map. Without that I think I would have been lost within minutes.

Swaying reeds rose above my head, cutting off all sight of the bungalows and the mat anchor lights. The only sound I could hear was the *slosh* of low waves slapping across the beach.

I reached the fence exactly when the d-box said I should. Instead of being nervous, all I could think of was how Colonel McFarlane would have a similar guidance display on his console, helping him navigate down to his destination.

I stopped by one of the posts with a warning sign. There was some kind of rough track on the other side, leading deeper in. According to the map in the d-box it would take me right up to one of the largest dump zones.

'I can't see any dogs,' Selim said.

'They're here,' I told him. 'Hang on a moment.' I keyed in the sound program I'd formatted. The portable terminal's speaker started to whistle, its high musical pitch rising and falling. I could just imagine the cold air flexing to carry the sound out over the reed clumps and stagnant pools in broad ripples.

We didn't have to wait long after that. Two huge Alsatians came racing down the track towards me. They flung themselves against the fence and tried to climb up, their forelegs scrabbling at the mesh. Their angry barking and snarling drowned out the whistling from my terminal.

Funnily enough, it was the other four who took a pace backwards when the dogs appeared. I remained where I was and took aim with the sonic jet. When I pressed the trigger the little gadget shook in my hand. It's supposed to fire a beam of sound in one direction; but even behind it I winced at what sounded like a banshee shrieking. For a horrible moment I thought I was holding it the wrong way round, and shooting myself! The sound that battered my ears (and they were covered by my Websuit visor, don't forget) was nothing to the one that must have hit the dogs. Both of them jumped back from the fence as if it had suddenly become electrified. They scrabbled round in the muddy soil yapping and whining, then they righted themselves and sprinted away.

My finger fell from the trigger. I could hear the dogs crashing through the undergrowth and splashing about in the shallow pools. They were so desperate to get clear they hadn't even bothered with the track.

'Wow! Venomous or what?' Selim shouted.

'It works,' Katie said. She sounded astonished, but delighted at the same time. 'It actually works.'

'Well done, Aynsley,' Bayliss said. 'That was brilliant. You were so cool.'

I didn't point out that there was a chain link fence between me and the dogs. Their admiration was doing wonders to my self-confidence. We were actually winning, and in Realworld, too, where it *meant* something.

They were all looking at me, waiting for me to say what was happening next. It felt wonderful. 'Let's go,' I told them. I rummaged round in my shoulder bag for the wire clippers.

It was tough cutting through the fence. Grass and weeds had woven themselves into the bottom. I had to really crouch down low to reach the links along the ground. It wasn't easy with all the layers of clothing I had on. Once I'd snipped out a wide horizontal gash I came back to the middle and sliced straight up for nearly two metres. After that I had to fold the two sides back as if they were tent flaps. It wasn't a simple thing to do. The wire was stiff and fought against everything I did to it.

Eventually, I had what I thought was a suitable gap.

'You could drive a lorry through that gap!' Selim exclaimed. 'Come on Aynsley, we've wasted ages while you cut this.'

It was tempting to tell him to curl up, but I resisted. Completing the mission properly was all that mattered. I moved forward cautiously, feeling the spikes of fence wire bending underneath me as I crossed over. I nearly fell, but just managed to shift my body weight back as I started to tip.

The others walked straight through the fence like ghosts, except for Katie. She made sure she used the gap I'd cut, stooping down to miss the ragged edges and everything. Selim sighed and shook his head at her.

'Aynsley went to a lot of trouble, and he's taking all the risk. The least we can do is show some support,' she said.

'All right,' Selim said grudgingly. 'Sorry, Aynsley.'

'That's OK.'

Katie grinned at me, and rolled her eyes heavenward. I grinned right back.

Now I was through, the first thing I did was make sure the coordinate of the gap was loaded into the navigation program. That way I could always find it again. No way did I want to have to cut another one.

According to the map, the big dump zone was another hundred and fifty metres away. The little track which was a clean straight green line in the d-box was in reality nothing more than a strip of grass which was lower than the reeds that formed a wall on either side of it. I started off down it, but the going was hard. I couldn't move very quickly.

'Keep looking out for any more dogs,' I told the others. It took all of my concentration to pick out a route through the tangled grass. My right hand gripped the sonic jet tightly.

'Can't you go any faster?' Selim grumbled.

'Hey, stop hassling him,' Drunlo said. 'Take all the time you need, Aynsley. This is fascinating.'

'I wasn't complaining, just asking.'

'It sounded like you were complaining.'

'Well, I wasn't, and I'm sorry if Aynsley thought so. And, anyway, what do you mean, "it's fascinating"?'

'Just look at it.' Drunlo swept his arms round in an extravagant gesture; he was smiling broadly. 'It's real and it's wild. Don't you love it?'

'Love it? It's a horrid little marsh! I bet it smells, too.'

I had wanted them along to provide company and support. Because, let's face it, venturing out into a dangerous well-guarded marsh in the middle of the night is not something I would ever do alone. Of course, back when we were dreaming up this mad stunt I had thought they *would* be supportive and helpful rather than spend the entire time bickering. Funny how your imagination can never quite get a good picture of what Realworld will actually be like. Grandpa calls that human nature.

'Dog coming!' Bayliss shouted.

'*Where?*' Panic turned my voice to a squeak.

'Front left.'

I was firing the sonic jet even before I'd aimed it properly. The dog was running through the reeds at the side of the track, which probably saved me. With those rigid, frozen, stalks in its way, it couldn't go anything like as fast as it could over open ground. I could see the reed clumps whipping about as if a small hurricane was ploughing through them. Then the dog's head burst through the frosty blades lining the path. Its jaws were parted wide enough to swallow my head in one bite. Fangs as big as my fingers were dripping saliva.

All I could do was shove the sonic jet in the dog's direction, the way priests are supposed to use a crucifix to ward off vampires. Every muscle I owned had gone rigid from fright.

The dog howled as the blast of sound struck it. I could see

the *anger* in its eyes. It shuddered from tip to tail, and crashed back into the reeds.

I was the one left shuddering then. I couldn't stop.

'It's gone, Aynsley,' Katie said. She was standing in front of me, looking anxiously at my face; one hand was resting on my shoulder. 'You're all right, you're safe.' Her fingers gave me a quick squeeze.

'It … it …' was all I could gasp.

Bayliss walked over to where the reeds had been flattened by the fleeing dog. 'I can't see it any more. I don't think that dog will stop before it reaches Wales.'

'What dog?' Selim asked. He was badly shaken. 'Did you see the size of it? That wasn't a dog, it was a sabre-toothed tiger!'

Drunlo nudged him, and frowned.

'Are you all right?' Katie asked.

'Yes.' I took a deep breath. 'Yes, I'm OK.'

'I couldn't have done that,' Bayliss said. 'Not in Real-world. I would have turned and tried to run. That was incredibly brave, Aynsley.'

'Thanks.'

'Listen,' Selim said. 'This isn't … Well, this trip isn't what I thought it was going to be like. If you want to turn round now, Aynsley, I'm going to be the one leading the way for you. Nobody's going to think you chickened out. Not after that dog. You could get badly hurt in here!'

The rest of them murmured their agreement.

It was tempting, I don't mind telling you. I checked the d-box. 'It's only seventy metres to the edge of the dump zone. That's too close after all we've done to get this far. I'm going to keep going. If another guard dog comes for me, then I'll probably turn round.' I faked up a smile. 'My nerves will probably be gone by then, anyway.'

'If that's what you want,' Katie said.

'Does the sonic jet have a power supply read-out?' Bayliss asked. He sounded very unhappy.

'Yes.'

'Perhaps you'd better check it. I don't know much about

them, but I think they're supposed to be fired in short bursts.'

I looked at the little gadget. Its power cell was down to twenty-three per cent. I really shouldn't have fired it for so long at that last dog. 'Oh, hell.' I looked from the power read-out to the d-box. Twenty-three per cent and seventy metres to go. 'Let's be quick,' I said. I started moving forward again.

This time there was no talk or squabbling. They all kept close to me as if clustering round would offer some form of protection. Pity I was the only one who could see them. If they were visible to the rest of the world, and if they'd worn some of the avatar forms we'd used in games, the demons, and wizards, and monster aliens, then no dog would ever have come near me.

'What's that?' Drunlo asked.

I pointed the sonic jet automatically, but managed not to press the trigger this time. Drunlo was looking at a patch of grass about five metres away.

'I don't see anything,' I said.

'I thought there was something moving about behind the clumps.'

'Another guard dog?' Bayliss asked.

'I'm not sure. It was smaller, I think.'

I remembered when I'd thought I'd seen a Web spider lurking in the marsh. And that was in broad daylight. Heavens only knew what an over-active imagination would find among the moonlight shadows.

'Fire the sonic jet at it,' Katie said. 'Then we'll know for sure.'

'If I do that I'll have to turn round now, I can't afford to waste the power. Besides, if it was a guard dog it wouldn't be hiding. We've seen that. It's probably just a fox or a pheasant.'

We waited for another half a minute, but nothing moved.

'Keep watching it,' I told Drunlo as I went on again.

The reeds began to thin out as I approached the dump

zone. I could hear a tiny stream trickling close by. Then the gas sensor began to bleep.

The sensor was one of the ideas Bayliss had had. I'd bought the unit from an electronics shop in King's Lynn. It's a standard commercial model which is mainly used in factories to warn the workers of any toxic fumes or gas leaks. Adapting it to detect hydrogen and methane was fairly simple. Bayliss and I found a technical site which showed us the auxiliary circuity and program we'd need to make it work. It only took ninety minutes to assemble the stack that it plugged into.

'Looks like we're here,' Bayliss said. He was studying the d-box which was displaying information from the gas sensor. 'There's not much hydrogen yet. Keep going forward Aynsley, let's see if it gets stronger.'

I held the sensor stack out in front of me, and looked ahead, I yelped in surprise. A woman was standing there looking at me.

CHAPTER NINE

SPIDERS IN THE MARSH

I suppose she was about the same age as Mum, I'm not very good at guessing adult ages. She was dressed in a dark suit with a high collar and gold buttons all the way up her front. It made her look terribly imperious, as if she were some kind of Grand Empress left over from the nineteenth century. A glimmer of green light shimmered off a ring she wore on her left index finger. Most memorable of all was her expression. Her contempt was far stronger then the guard dog's. She seemed to regard the world around her with utter disgust.

She vanished. Just that, and nothing more. She didn't walk away, she didn't crouch down in the reeds. She just vanished.

'Who was that?' Katie asked in a scared whisper.

'Where did she go?' Drunlo asked.

'Quiet!' I yelled. 'Did everyone see her?'

They all said yes.

'But we couldn't have done,' Bayliss said. 'Not *seen* her. She vanished faster than an avatar that has scuttled. That means she couldn't be real; actual people can't do that.'

'A ghost could,' Selim said.

He flinched as Katie and Bayliss glared at him.

'Sorry,' he said guiltily. 'It was just an idea.'

The trouble was, exactly the same idea had already popped up in my mind. With it came a cold sensation that crept inside my coat to prickle my skin. 'Ghosts aren't real,' I said. 'She was something else.' I think I was mostly trying to convince myself.

'Absolutely, she wasn't a ghost,' Katie said.

'So what is she?' Drunlo asked. 'And more importantly, where is she now?'

'Let's think this through logically,' Bayliss said in his most serious voice. 'No real person could vanish like that, only an avatar. That must mean what we saw was some kind of avatar.'

'But this is a personal communication channel,' I said. 'I didn't spin the terminal into a public site. Nobody else should be able to get in and join us.'

'It's probably just a funnelled hook-up,' Selim said. 'Let's face it, tonight of all nights the communication circuits are going to be operating close to maximum capacity. There's bound to be some mistakes.'

'Could be,' Bayliss said grudgingly.

'I didn't like the way she looked at us,' Katie said. 'It was as if she knew us.'

'Well, did anybody recognize her, then?' I asked.

Nobody did.

'That means nothing,' Selim pointed out. 'If it was an avatar, it could have been anyone. It doesn't even have to be a woman.'

'So who could it have been? Who would be interested in us?'

'The police, for a start. Or someone from Bigene Industrie's security division,' Bayliss said. 'In which case it might not be an accident she appeared in our communication channel. After all, we broke into their company data storage; I'm sure they can do the same thing to us.'

'So what do we do?' Drunlo asked.

'I'll tell you exactly,' I said forcefully. 'I scoop up some algae, and we get out of this marsh, *pronto*.'

'Good idea.'

I was four or five metres from the edge of a big pool, one of the largest I'd found in the marsh, fifteen metres across at least. What with the woman appearing, I hadn't really noticed the smell in the air. It was a pong like milk that's been left out in the sun for a week. The gas sensor d-box was telling me that all sorts of chemicals were floating about in the air.

While the others kept watch for dogs or in case the woman came back I fished round in my shoulder bag for a torch. The light amplification program was fine, but it made the surface of the pool look like a silver mirror. With the torch beam on, everything reverted to its genuine colour. The surface of the pool wasn't even water. It was covered in a thick layer of hideous grey-green sludge with the texture of rice pudding. Tiny bubbles were bulging up everywhere, as if the algae was developing blisters. When they were as big as my thumbnail they'd burst open with a soft squelching sound. All the vegetation growing around the edge had turned a sickly yellow. The reeds were wilting, their thick stems flopping over to melt into the algae.

'Yuck!' Katie exclaimed. 'It's disgusting.'

'Think yourself lucky you can't smell it,' I told her.

I moved over to the edge. There was a dead frog lying on the top of of the algae. When I looked further across the pond I could see other frogs half-submerged in the tacky green sludge. Several small birds had also been claimed.

I hated Bigene Industrie for being so cheap. What earthly difference would it make to the finances of a company that size if they'd waited a few weeks until the ultraviolet processor had arrived? Because they were so petty-minded, innocent creatures were dying in what was supposed to be their refugee. As if we didn't have enough death in the world, they had to add to it for the sake of share prices.

'Come on, Aynsley,' Bayliss urged quietly. 'We need to get out of here.'

'Right.' I rummaged through the shoulder bag until I found the scoop I'd built. Nothing special, just a glass jar attached to an aluminium pole. I'd thought it would allow me to reach blobs of algae in case they were floating out of reach. I hadn't expected so much of the stuff!

I stretched forwards, dipping the jar into the algae. A spider emerged from the withered reeds on the other side of the pool, and started pattering over the surface towards me.

The wretched thing must have been a metre across, with a skin that was patterned in jagged green and yellow stripes. I recognized it instantly, one of Bigene Industrie's guardian spiders from inside their headquarters.

'This isn't happening!' Selim cried.

'Oh, yes it is!' Baylis said. 'The company has intercepted our communications. They're coming after us.'

Even as he said it, I knew there was something wrong about the situation. For the life of me, I couldn't think what. And I did have something that required more urgent attention!

Another spider emerged from the verge behind the first, then a third.

'What do we do?' Selim shouted.

'Leave!' I shouted back. I dropped the algae jar. I dropped the torch. I dropped the shoulder bag. Anything to lighten the load. All I had left was the portable terminal and the sonic jet.

I reversed away from the pool fast, then spun round and shot off down the overgrown path.

'Aynsley, this is no good,' Bayliss cried. 'The spiders aren't back at the pool, they've infiltrated your terminal's link with the Web. You can't outrun them, not physically.'

I looked over my shoulder, and sure enough the spiders were still with us. In fact they were closer now (or should that be larger?). Another two had appeared, making five of them now.

'What do I do?' I yelped. I still didn't stop moving, though.

'They're obviously here to wreck our communications. They must want to funnel your terminal. That way, we'll be separated.'

'Don't let them. Please!' I was really scared now. Without the terminal I'd be alone, and lost.

'How do we stop them?' Katie asked.

'They're only programs,' Bayliss replied. 'Hostile phaces, that's all. Let's try some of our games weapons.' His avatar flickered as he tapped at his suit keyboard. Then he was mutating, his ordinary shirt and jeans darkening into army combat fatigues; grey anti-projectile armour clipped itself around his limbs and torso, a helmet covered in electronic antennae swung down over his head. A fully tooled-up Centauri starship marine was running beside me. He turned, levelling his laser carbine at the leading spider, and fired. A violet laser beam stabbed out, its heavy power rating making the air sizzle. The spider imploded, warping into a fuzzy multicoloured bauble that swiftly turned black. Then it was gone.

'Wowieee!' Selim bellowed. 'Way to go, Major Bayliss, sir.' He began to change, transforming into a silver-grey robot warrior with magnetic cannons where his hands should be. I thought I recognized it out of the *Hellhunter Squad* game.

Bayliss fired another two laser blasts, sending a couple more spiders into oblivion. 'We must stop them from reaching Aynsley,' he said. 'Don't let them touch him.'

The robot warrier's cannons pounded a fusillade of blazing shells into a spider. It burst apart in a blizzard of pixels that twirled away over the marsh like leaves in a winter wind.

For every spider destroyed another appeared behind me, sometimes two.

Katie charged past me, looking quite splendid in her elf princess forest costume, long chestnut hair flowing over her shoulders. She swung a long silver staff over her head, and brought it crashing down on a spider.

Drunlo hadn't changed. But he had armed himself with a crossbow. Darts of scarlet light flew from it, puncturing spiders as if they were balloons.

They must have dispatched over twenty spiders between them before their weapons began to lose power. When Bayliss fired his laser, the beam struck a spider and broke apart into a spray of sparks. The spider juddered under the impact, but kept on coming. It was as if the laser had become nothing worse than a jet of water.

'They're adapting!' Bayliss shouted. 'We have to alter.'

His marine armour gave way to a soldier in a World War One khaki battle dress. He took careful aim with his Enfield rifle, and shot the spider. It exploded into a fog of emerald stars.

Katie became an Eastern assassin, clad from head to toe in black robes. A viciously sharp dagger with a long curving blade sprouted from her hand. She swiped it across a spider's head, decapitating it completely. 'Yes! Easy,' she yelled.

There were more spiders than ever now. Ten or fifteen of them circling us, gradually creeping closer. My protectors were slowly being squeezed in. Plasma beams and magic swords were flashing around me like a barrage of small lightning bolts. Despite the distraction, I was still on course for the gap in the fence. It was only ten metres away now. I could actually see one of the posts.

I didn't know quite what would happen when I was through; whether the spiders would stop or keep on coming for me. I didn't really care after that. Once I was on the other side, it was a straight run home. Nothing else mattered.

A spider wriggled out of the reeds ahead of me. It was different to the others, smaller, perhaps twenty centimetres across, with dark scaly lizard-like skin. There was a small metallic disk on the top of its head. For a crazy moment I thought it was balancing a coin there.

Katie leaped forwards, and stabbed at it. Her knife went straight through without having any effect.

'Hell!' she swore. Her image altered. A Queen Witch stood between me and the dark spider, ermine-lined cloak flapping in the wind, a single gold band crowning her flaming red hair. She raised her wand a crystal baton with blue static flaring along its length, and uttered a spell. Green light squirted down to engulf the dark spider. It had no effect whatsoever!

'No,' Katie grunted. Then she frowned, and walked right up to the spider. It took no notice of her. 'Aynsley, I think—'

She bent down and reached out. Her hand passed straight through it. 'Aynsley! It's real!'

'It can't be,' Bayliss shouted.

Katie had jumped back as if her hand had been burned. 'It is, it's real. Aynsley, get away. Just run.'

I stared at the dark spider in horror. Two more were emerging on to the path beside it.

'Run, Aynsley. Run!'

A cruel laugh rang out in the night air. 'Oh, my dears, that's the one thing poor Aynsley can never do.'

The woman materialized right in front of me. She was older this time, even more imposing. Her lips twisted into a mocking sneer. 'He's fooled all of you, you know. He's lied to you the whole time.'

She stretched out her left arm. A pale gold ring with a large red stone on it was sitting on her index finger. It touched my shoulder. I never felt a thing.

My portable terminal let out a wild bleep.

I knew what she'd done without having to consult any management d-box. A wordless cry came out of my lips. There was nothing I could do to stop it. I looked down to see the avatar program crashing. Pixels rained away from my jeans and sturdy boots to show what was really there. Now they could all see the powered wheelchair with its worn-down tyres coated in mud. My useless legs were wrapped in a tartan rug against the cold; while my feet were shoved into quilted thermal socks that velcro straps held securely in place on the rest plates.

'Aynsley!' Katie gasped. The tone was full of astonishment and sorrow.

The other three simply stared dumbly.

I was still rolling forward, the motors making hard work of the thick tangled grass. One of the dark spiders darted under a wheel. Before I could brake, the wheelchair was trying to ride over the spider's bloated body. It started to tip over. I flung my weight deserately the other way, but it was already too late. The wheelchair overturned, spilling me out on to the icy grass.

CHAPTER TEN

THE BIGGEST LIGHTSTORM
IN THE WORLD, EVER

My eyes were tight shut. I knew the others would be looking at me, and I didn't want to see them. In my mind I could see their expressions of pity and embarrassment. It's always there the first time people see me. After that, after the first time, when they're used to me, I become an irritation, the one everybody else has to wait for, or make allowances for. The one who can't join in. The alien. The victim. The target.

'He doesn't trust you with the truth about himself,' the woman said. 'He doesn't trust you with many things. His whole life is a figment of lies. I'm afraid I have to tell you, poor Aynsley is not a very nice little boy. Not nice at all.'

'Why are you saying this?' Bayliss asked. 'Who are you?'

'I am a security procedure Bigene Industrie employs,' she said calmly. 'You remember them? The company whose land Aynsley is busy trespassing on right this minutes. Whose files he infected with dangerous viruses. By the way, you'll be happy to hear we didn't lose too much medical research data. Our new biologically produced medicine will still be available to cure people on schedule next year.'

'Medicines?' Katie asked.

'Yes, medicines. Those program viruses are quite indiscriminate in what they wreck. I take it you did know about them?'

'I knew,' she whispered. 'We caught a cyberat.'

'Of course. But it would be Aynsley who roped you in; Aynsley who infected our storage space. Am I right?

'Yes.'

'I thought so. Aynsley's family is very familiar with these matters. He does come from a criminal background after all. I expect that was another of the things about himself he neglected to mention.'

'He never said,' Bayliss agreed meekly.

'No. Well, his Uncle Elton is a convicted anarchist who's currently in jail. Not someone you brag about when you're trying to fool your friends into following you. Frankly, I'm rather glad you didn't allow yourself to get involved too deeply in his schemes. I expect that means we won't be taking you to court.'

'Court!'

'Yes.' Her voice sounded very patient. 'You have been committing some very serious crimes. Are you saying you think you are above the law?'

'No. But—'

'But what?'

'Well, we only did this because we thought Bigene Industrie had dumped some algae here illegally.'

'Oh dear, Aynsley really did twist the facts around to suit himself, didn't he? We are fully aware that some of our solar mat algae is still alive. This marsh was a pioneering scheme. We never claimed it would be perfect. As it happens, the sterilization method we employed wasn't a hundred per cent effective. It's most regrettable, but that's life. However, because of this minor malfunction, we now know how to make the procedure work correctly. Trial and error has formed the basis of our society for centuries, it is the way humans progress. Currently, we're trying to neutralize the algae which escaped. It's a very difficult job, and given that the algae gives off a potentially explosive gas, a dangerous one, too. That's why this whole area of marshland is fenced off.'

'Why didn't you warn people? Why the secrecy?

'We were trying to do it quietly and efficiently. If people thought the marsh was going to blow up, there would be a panic. Heacham would become a ghost town, nobody would visit. The local economy would be destroyed, which would cost dozens of jobs. We don't want to be responsible for that, too.'

'They wouldn't think it was dangerous unless it was.'

'I wish you were right. Unfortunately, the media loves to exaggerate. If one report says a minor technical problem is being dealt with, and another says explosive gas is leaking out of the ground, which do you think will be put on the news site? Which will have the higher access rate? Which will earn the news company the most money? Yes, they are both true; however, it's in their interest to push the most dramatic of the two. You've seen what happens when someone doesn't present the facts accurately. Because here you all are on an illegal wild goose chase when you should be spinning in to the GSA's Olympus site for the Mars landing like the rest of the planet.'

'The algae problem is really under control?' Selim asked.

'Of course it is. We know where the dump zones are, and we'll have them neutralized in another six months. This marsh is scheduled to be opened in another year or so. We'd hardly publicize that if we weren't doing anything about it, now would we?'

It was all so convincing. She had an answer for each question, each nagging problem. Everything I'd done, everything I'd said, was all wrong. Even I was doubting me. That smooth voice made it sound so plausible.

The expressions would be changing, just like they always did. Their pity giving way to exasperation and annoyance. In this case there would be betrayal as well. I was the one who'd brought them here, the one who had actively got them into trouble. Unless of course the woman was kind to them and didn't press charges. Which she would be, providing they were suitably apologetic. The lesson would be learned, and they wouldn't do anything like this again. Ever. They certainly wouldn't have anything more to do with me. Nobody would spin in tomorrow to chase this fade.

The woman had separated me from their friendship as

effectively as I was separated from them physically. In a minute I was going to be completely alone, apart from her.

I heard something shuffle through the grass next to me, and opened my eyes. One of the dark spiders was dragging my sonic jet away. It was already out of my reach. The disk of metal on its head was glinting dimly in the moonlight. I squinted, trying to get a better look.

'The spiders,' I said faintly.

The woman glanced down at me. 'Be quiet, Aynsley. You're in enough trouble as it is.'

'The spiders. What are they? Katie, Selim, Bayliss, Drunlo, please, just ask her. Please!'

'Be quiet, Aynsley,' the woman said. Her voice had become quite sharp.

The four of them looked at each other silently. Bayliss and Katie were frowning.

'Yes, what are they?' Bayliss said. He had turned to watch the one with my sonic jet.

'They're just robots,' the woman said. 'Part of our security procedures.'

'No, they're not robots,' I said. 'They're alive. Look at the one that got squashed under my wheelchair. They're living, but they're not natural.'

'Rubbish. They're designed to be as lifelike as possible, that's all.'

Baylis had squatted down beside the sticky pulp of the squashed spider. 'Aynsley's right.' He glanced up at the woman. 'This isn't a robot.'

'And look how they're controlled,' I said. 'That disk on their head.'

'What have you done?' Katie asked. 'What are these things?'

'Robots,' the woman insisted sternly. 'It's just plastic, that's all.'

Katie walked up to her, and shook her head. 'No. I see what you're trying to do now. You're trying to get us to abandon Aynsley. I didn't think he would lie to us. I know him too well.'

'You know nothing about him, my girl. You didn't even know he was disabled.'

'I didn't need to know he was disabled. That's part of Realworld, it's physical. Friendship isn't physical, it's all about personality. That's the beauty of the Web, you can't hide your true self here. You have to be honest with your thoughts, you have to talk to people. We know our avatars are false. It's not what you look like that counts, it's who you are, what you say that matters. Aynsley's a bit shy, he talks like a nerd some times, and he's obsessed with spaceflight, but that doesn't make him bad. He's not a liar, not with us. I believe him. I believe your company is trying to cover up the algae. And now I *know* you've been conducting some horrible experiment on these awful spiders.'

'Katie's right,' Selim said. He came over to stand by me. 'Aynsley is one of us. Besides ...' His lips twitched in a regretful smile. I could see him typing something on his suit keypad. The avatar with perfect skin and handsome features vanished. I knew it was his realoe that took its place, he had the same smile. But this boy was big. I don't mean like a sports-type, all healthy weight and broad shoulders. I mean fat.

'You see,' Selim said. 'If you think Aynsley lied, then so did I. All of us do in Realworld, we have to; it makes life comfortable and gets us through the day. But in here we're all equal. If we get on in here, it's because we genuinely like each other. Aynsley's my friend. He wouldn't leave me. I won't leave him.'

'Nor me,' Bayliss said. He came over to stand next to Selim.

Drunlo grinned. 'That makes four of us.'

'Well, well,' the woman said. The original contempt had returned to her face. 'What a pitiful collection of misfits. Stay together if you want. It makes no difference to me. I'll have you all sent to a secure remand home together. The crimes you've committed are still real enough.'

'Not as big as yours, though,' Drunlo said.

The woman stiffened, looking at him suspiciously.

'Aynsley and Selim aren't the only ones who kept quiet about their nature,' Drunlo said. 'I did, too.'

'How tiresome,' the woman sneered. 'And what misfortune are you hiding? Are you missing an arm, or have you got some illness we're all supposed to be sorry and sympathetic about?'

'No. Nothing like that.' Drunlo laughed happily. 'I'm not human.'

'Drunlo!' Katie spluttered.

'I'm from Lilliput,' he said. 'I used to be a phace in the GulliverZone. Then we became self aware. We were granted UN citizenship this February.'

Even though I was lying on my side on the freezing ground, with my arms bent painfully, I forgot how uncomfortable I was and just stared at him. 'You're biting us!'

'No, I'm not, Aynsley.'

Then I remembered how bewitched he was with the bungalows and the field when I switched my Websuit to provider mode. Of course he would be! Realworld would be as wonderful and exciting and different to him as the Web sites were to us.

'You're human, Drunlo,' Katie said. 'Just as human as we are. You simply don't have a biological body, that's all.'

'That's quite an irony, isn't it?' Drunlo said.

I didn't like this tone, it was too steady and polite, the way people speak when they're really angry. He and the woman hadn't stopped staring at each other.

'You still haven't told us your name,' he said. 'Not that you have to. I saw you once before, when you were masquerading as Queen of Lilliput. Isn't that right, Sorceress?'

All of us turned to look at her. I felt the same kind of fear as I had when the dogs were running at me. The Sorceress! The greatest Webcriminal there had ever been. A woman who hunted Realworld and the sites for people to experiment on.

I whimpered loudly when I realized how close I had come

to being left alone with her. 'Don't leave me,' I breathed to the others. 'Not now.'

'We're here, Aynsley,' Katie said fiercely. 'She won't get you, she won't get any of us.'

'No,' the Sorceress said. 'I won't have you, Aynsley. Not now. But the guard dogs will.'

'I'll call for help,' Bayliss said.

The Sorceress laughed viciously. 'Call away, nobody will get here in time. This is a squalid little marsh in a nowhere county. It'll take them hours to find him.'

I shifted round on the ground to search for the dark spider that had my sonic jet. The vile thing was squirming back into the thick reeds, dragging the gadget with it. When I tried to crawl after it my feet stopped me from moving more than a few centimetres. They were still strapped into the wheelchair.

Somewhere in the distance, a dog was howling.

'I'm going to make sure you're alone when they get here,' the Sorceress hissed. 'No friends to comfort you, Aynsley. You face the dogs all by yourself, crying and pleading to the empty air. That's your punishment for raiding my scheme.'

Web spiders were emerging behind her. They started to march forward.

'Weapons!' Selim called. His podgy realoe was replaced by a tall knight in brilliant silver armour. He raised a golden sword. 'All for one!' he roared as he launched himself at the spiders.

Drunlo fought at his side, his body alight in a halo of red fire. Any spider he touched shrivelled into grey ash. Katie had become a huge dark werewolf, her fierce jaws snapping spider bodies to pieces. Bayliss was in a yellow space suit, firing his atomic ray pistol.

I struggled with the velcro straps around my feet. Fear and speed making the task ten times more difficult than it should be.

Katie was the first to succumb. The spiders overwhelmed her, piling on from every side. Her furry body disappeared beneath them. 'You're my friend, Aynsley,' she called out before she was engulfed.

I still hadn't freed my straps. The dog howled again. It was louder this time. Even if Katie alerted the police *right now* they wouldn't get here in time. Nobody would. I was going down the plug, permanently.

Bayliss was next. A spider sneaked up behind him, and clamped its legs round his neck. The pair of them melted into a whirling tornado of yellow pixels that drilled its way into the earth.

I stopped tugging at the twisted straps. It was useless. I needed someone close by to come to the rescue. Mum! Mum always made me carry the mobile phone in case I got into trouble. I'd even brought it with me tonight, putting it into the shoulder bag automatically.

I'd dropped the shoulder bag in a panic when the first Web spider emerged. I started sobbing.

Two spiders landed on Drunlo. His flames went out, then his entire body was extinguished. A fountain of hissing steam jetted up at the stars.

Selim pushed his spacesuit helmet visor up. He looked straight at me, his face crumpled up in anguish. Tears were rolling down his cheeks. 'Aynsley!'

The dog was barking now. I could hear it crashing though the reeds as it sprinted towards me.

There were no sticks lying around I could use to beat it off with. I had nothing left. It was the end. Then I remembered why I was here, what crazy crusade had lured me out to this marsh in the first place. The lightstorms.

'Phone me!' I screamed. 'Selim, phone me! Me! PHONE.'

His mouth began to part, whether to voice bewilderment or understanding I never knew. He scuttled before the last five spiders pounced.

'I won,' the Sorceress said triumphantly. 'You're all alone.'

I rolled on to my back to see her looking down at me. Her smile was as cold and treacherous as black ice.

My mobile phone rang.

I could just hear it, shrilling away to itself where I'd dropped the shoulder bag at the edge of the pool. The pool that was leaking hydrogen.

The Sorceress heard it too. She swung round and shouted a furious: 'NO!'

That sign at the garage was quite right; you really should switch phones off when there's gas about.

The marsh exploded.

CHAPTER ELEVEN

LANDING ON A
NEW WORLD

Events got a little mixed up in my mind. The doctors said that was due to mild concussion.

The worst part of the explosion was the sound. It was like being on the receiving end of a sonic boom. Actually, no, I take that back. The worst part was the blast wave. It picked me clean off the ground and threw me into the reeds. Because my feet were still strapped to the wheelchair I dislocated both ankles during my short flight. It's the first time I've been grateful I don't have any feeling below my waist. You should see how big they swelled up!

I never did see that last guard dog. Not for lack of light. Half of the sky turned blinding white.

That first explosion was so big it triggered off a chain reaction across nearly all the marsh's dump zones. Heacham's entire population came running out of their homes to see blue-white streamers of flame zooming up into the night. Someone said it was like a firework display that was using nuclear rockets.

I was lying there in a bit of a state for twenty minutes before the rescue party found me. My friends told the police where I was. This time, people listened.

Mum and Dad were frantic when they found I wasn't in my cocoon. They got an even worse shock when Katie phoned them.

I still feel guilty about that.

But I did get to fly! A genuine flight in a helicopter. They airlifted me to King's Lynn hospital.

That was when I got to meet Ariadne, the Korean

Webcop assigned to track down the Sorceress. She'd arrived in the helicopter from London where her team were liaising with the Criminal Intelligence Bureau. Apparently, they knew the Sorceress was in Europe, though they didn't know what she was doing here.

Ariadne flew with me to the hospital, asking all sorts of questions. I don't remember many of them. She was *very* interested in the dark spiders, though.

It was Drunlo who contacted her. He knew her from back when the Webcops chased the Sorceress in GulliverZone.

Arriving at the hospital is a complete blank. Same for the next ten hours.

I woke up to find Mum and Dad asleep on a couch next to my bed. My legs were all wrapped up in thick dressings. I had cuts and bruises everywhere. And I *really* don't want to talk about how I have to go to the toilet.

Mum cried a lot, and held my hand tight the whole time she tore into me about how stupid I'd been. Dad was quieter, angry and frightened. I got the whole you-should-come-to-us-with-any-problems lecture. I nodded and said I would in future. I didn't tell them about the way the kids from the other bungalows treat me, I think I've upset them enough for now.

The doctor and a couple of nurses came in after that. He told me that there was nothing wrong with me, apart from my ankles, and he was only keeping me in for forty-eight hours for observation because of my suspected concussion.

I was allowed to have lunch in peace, although the nurse who brought it told me the hospital was under siege by reporters. When she opened the door to my room, I caught a glimpse of two uniformed police officers standing outside.

After lunch, Ariadne visited. She looked me up and down with a sly smile, then pulled a chair over to the side of the bed.

'You're looking better than you did last night. Aynsley.'

'Thank you.'

'That was quite a little escapade you spun into there.'

'Yes. Um, am I under arrest?

'No. Nor will any charges be brought against you. Not by us, and certainly not by Bigene Industrie.'

'They won't?' I asked in surprise.

'Oh no. They've had quite enough bad publicity as it is. Taking children to court for revealing how badly they'd been infiltrated by the Sorceress would make it ten times worse for them.'

I smiled. It was the first one of the day.

'That's how Realworld works, Aynsley. Appearance and image means a lot out there.' She gestured at the window.

'What did you mean about the Sorceress infiltrating Bigene Industrie?'

'My team have been doing a lot of research since last night. You see, the Sorceress is a very wealthy woman, her involvement with the Web and multimedia corporations has earned her a lot of money over the last few decades. She used some of it to buy a big block of Bigene Industrie's shares, enough to get her a seat on its board of directors. That allowed her to control one of its subsidiary divisions outright, and influence several others.'

'Which division did she control?'

'It was the division that developed the jockey chip. You know, like the one Colonel McFarlane is using.'

'I know. Why did she want to be in charge of that?'

'You've heard the rumours about her? She's an old woman who's now very frightened of dying. She wants to transfer her mind into the Web where she'll go on living for ever. Jockey chip technology brings that possibility a step closer because it can actually connect the nervous system directly into electronic networks. Unfortunately, when she took over the Bigene Industrie development division the technology was at a very early stage, and the Sorceress is an impatient woman with her own very special timetable. She diverted hundreds of millions of Euros into perfecting the jockey chip. That's why the ultraviolet machine to sterilize mat algae was late in arriving. The company's finances were

in a complete mess by that time. Heacham marsh was only
one of the casualties.'

'Can she do that? Can she transfer her mind into the
Web now?'

'I don't know, is the honest answer. She's already used
jockey chip technology in a way it was never intended.'

'The dark spiders!' I exclaimed.

'That's right. The little disk on their heads was a modified
jockey chip. She could control their brains with it.'

I shivered. 'What were those spiders?'

'Rather gruesome artificial creatures that had been put
together by another Bigene Industrie laboratory she was
running. It was supposed to have been researching organ
transplants. They were made up from parts of other
animals.'

'That's disgusting!'

'You should spin in to the Frankenstein site some day, or
perhaps even read the original book by Mary Shelley.
Stitching different body parts together is a very old idea. It
just takes someone with a mind as warped as hers to make
it work.'

'Will you catch her?'

'I hope so. I think her time is running out. She's
becoming quite desperate these days, which means she's
starting to make mistakes. Five years ago, she would never
have left a loose end like the marsh for anyone to discover.
I'm close to her now, very close. It's only going to take one
more blunder on her part, and we'll have her. You should
be very proud of what you've done, she's a step closer to
justice now.'

I remember what Selim had said, what seemed like years
ago. 'Is there a reward?'

Ariadne laughed. 'No there isn't! Do you know how
much damage you caused? Heacham doesn't have a marsh
any more, it looks like a bomb hit it. The government will
have to spend hundreds of thousands of Euros repairing
and replanting it. That money has to come from hard-
pressed taxpayers.'

'Oh. I'm sorry.' I could feel the warm blush rising up my cheeks.

'I should think so, too. However, some of us do appreciate what you did.' She clicked open the briefcase she'd brought with her, and pulled out a brand new, top-of-the-range, portable terminal. 'Our discretionary fund can run to this,' she said, and plonked it down on the blanket. 'Your old terminal was a complete write-off.'

'This is for me?'

Yes.' She began producing various ancillary modules, a gag set, and hardcubes of add-on programs. 'I've loaded your e-mail address space with my private code. One, don't ever do anything like this again. Two, if you do find any crime being committed in the Web, call me.'

'I promise.'

'Thank heavens for that. We don't want you turning out like your wicked Uncle Elton, now do we.'

My blush deepened.

Ariadne stood up and grinned. Then she planted a kiss on my forehead. Thank heavens no one else was in the room, it was more embarrassing than when Grandpa hugs me.

'The Sorceress was right about one thing, you'll be happy to hear.'

'What's that?' I asked.

'Things don't always go right first time. Take last night, a fuel pump failed in the Olympus landing craft. It meant they delayed the flight down to the surface by a day.'

My mouth dropped open and I gaped at her dumbly.

Ariadne winked as she walked out of the door. 'Take care, Aynsley.'

I tore at the polythene wrapping round the glove and glasses set, and plugged it into the portable terminal. A trapdoor opened in the floor, and Drunlo jumped out. 'It took you long enough,' he moaned.

Selim's landing pod sank out of the sky to hover just outside the window. The top hinged open, and he hopped over on to the open window ledge. 'Hi, Aynsley. How are you feeling? I watched the marsh explosion a dozen times today on the news sites. It was *venomous*.'

'It felt venomous, too.'

Katie and Bayliss opened the door and walked in.

'Does it hurt?' Bayliss asked.

Katie pulled a face at him behind his back.

'Only if I laugh.'

'We showed those spiders, didn't we,' Drunlo said.

'Certainly did.'

'My *Hellhunter Squad* robot was the best for dealing with them. I raided no end with that avatar.'

'Curl up! My crossbow got at least fifty!'

'No way.'

Katie sat on the edge of my bed. 'Looks like this fade is going to take a very long time to chase.'

'I think you're right.'

'Aynsley?' Drunlo asked cautiously.

'My legs?' I guessed.

'If you don't want to talk about it … I just thought doctors can cure most things you people get.'

'Us people,' Katie told him softly.

He smiled gratefully at her.

'It's a nervous disorder. Very rare. The neuro-specialist says they can probably treat it once I've stopped growing. Five more years.'

'That's not so long,' Selim said. 'And look what you've achieved already.'

'Thanks. And that was some fast dialing you did last night.'

He beamed. 'Easy.'

'Did Ariadne say if the Webcobs found any of those dark spiders?' Drunlo asked.

'Can it wait a minute?' I asked. 'I really don't want to miss the Mars landing this time. We can access all of it today.'

They gave in with good grace, and I spun us into the GSA site. Colonel McFarlane was just shutting the airlock hatch. He swam through the landing craft to the cockpit and began strapping himself into the pilot's seat. Mars was a beautiful red crescent waiting expectantly outside the narrow windscreen. If such extraordinary events could happen right outside my own door, I wondered what could possibly be waiting for the colonel down there.

'I've been counting,' Bayliss said. 'You know, I shot seventeen Web spiders with my atomic pistol.'

'Bayliss!'

WEBSPEAK – A GLOSSARY

AI	Artificial intelligence. Computer programs that appear to show intelligent behaviour when you interact with them.
avatar or realoe	Personas in the Web that are the representations of real people.
basement-level	Of the lowest level possible. Often used as an insult, as in 'You've got a basement-level grasp of the situation.'
bat	The moment of transition into the Web or between sites. You can 'do a bat' or 'go bat'. Its slang use has extended to the everyday world. 'bat' is used instead of 'come in', 'take a bat' is a dismissal. (From *Blue And Tone*.)
bite	To play a trick, or to get something over on someone.
bootstrap	Verb, to improve your situation by your own efforts.
bot	Programs with AI.
chasing the fade	Analysing what has happened in the Web after you have left it.
cocoon	A secret refuge, also your bed or own room.
cog	Incredibly boring or dull. Initially specific to the UK and America this slang is now in use worldwide. (From *Common Or Garden* spider.)

curl up	'Go away, I don't like you!' (From *curl up and die*.)
cyberat	A Web construct, a descendent of computer viruses, that infests the Web programs.
cybercafe	A place where you can get drinks and snacks as well as renting time in the Web.
cyberspace	The visual representation of the communication system which links computers.
d-box	A data-box; an area of information which appears when people are in Virtual Reality (VR).
download	To enter the Web without leaving a Realworld copy.
down the plug	A disaster, as in 'We were down the plug'.
egg	A younger sibling or annoying hanger-on. Even in the first sense this is always meant nastily.
eight	Good (a spider has eight legs).
flame	An insult or nasty remark.
fly	A choice morsel of information, a clue, a hint.
funnel	An unexpected problem or obstacle.
gag	Someone, or something, you don't like very much, who you consider to be stupid. (From *Glove And Glasses*.)
glove and glasses	Cheap but outdated system for experiencing Virtual Reality. The glasses allow you to see VR, the gloves allow you to pick things up.
Id	Interactive display nodule.
mage	A magician.
mip	Measure of computer power.
nick or alias	A nickname. For example, 'Metaphor' is the nickname of Sarah.

one-mip   Of limited worth or intelligence, as in 'a one-mip mind'.

phace   A person you meet in the Web who is not real; someone created by the software of a particular site or game.

phreak   Someone who is fanatical about virtual reality experiences in the Web.

protocol   The language one computer uses to talk to another.

raid   Any unscheduled intrusion into the Web; anything that forces someone to leave; a program crash.

realoe   See *avatar*.

Realworld   What it says; the world outside the Web. Sometimes used in a derogatory way.

scuttle   Leave the Web and return to the Realworld.

silky   Smarmy, over enthusiastic, untrustworthy.

six   Bad (an insect has six legs).

slows, the   The feeling that time has slowed down after experiencing the faster time of the Web.

spider   A web construct. Appearing in varying sizes and guises, these are used to pass on warnings or information in the Web. The word is also commonly applied to teachers or parents.

spidered-off   Warned away by a spider.

spin in   To enter the Web or a Website.

spin out   To leave the Web or a Website.

SFX   Special effects.

strand   A gap between rows of site skyscrapers in Webtown. Used to describe any street or road or journey.

suck   To eat or drink.

supertime   Parts of the Web that run even faster

	than normal.
TFO	Tennessee Fried Ostrich.
venomous	Adjective; excellent; could be used in reference to piece of equipment (usually a Websuit) or piece of programming.
vets	Veterans of any game or site. Ultra-vets are the *crème de la crème* of these.
VR	Virtual Reality. The illusion of a three dimensional reality created by computer software.
warlock	A sorcerer; magician.
Web	The worldwide network of communication links, entertainment, educational and administrative sites that exists in cyberspace and is represented in Virtual Reality.
Web heads	People who are fanatical about surfing the Web. (See also phreaks.)
Web round	Verb; to contact other Web users via the Web.
Websuit	The all over body suit lined with receptors which when worn by Web users allows them to experience the full physical illusion of virtual reality.
Webware	Computer software used to create and/or maintain the Web.
widow	Adjective; excellent; the term comes from the Black Widow, a particularly poisonous spider.
wipeout	To be comprehensively beaten in a Web game or to come out worse in any Web situation.

OTHER TITLES IN
THE WEB SERIES

GULLIVERZONE by Steve Baxter

February 7, 2027, World Peace Day. It's a day of celebration everywhere. Even access to the Web is free today. It's the chance Sarah's been waiting for, a chance to sample the most wicked sites, to visit mind-blowing virtual worlds. She chooses GulliverZone and the chance to be a giant amongst the tiny people of Lilliput.

But the peace that is being celebrated in the real world does not extend into cyberspace. There is a battle for survival being fought in Lilliput and what Sarah discovers there in one day will be enough to change her life for ever – providing she can get out to live it ...

GULLIVERZONE, the fear is anything but virtual.

GULLIVERZONE ready for access.

FEEL UP TO ANOTHER?

DREAMCASTLE by Stephen Bowkett

Dreamcastle is the premier fantasy role-playing site on the Web, and Surfer is one of the premier players. He's one of the few to fight his way past the 500th level, one of the few to take on the Stormdragon and win. But it isn't enough, Surfer has his eyes on the ultimate prize. He wants to be the best, to discover the dark secret at the core of Dreamcastle. And he's found the girl to take him there. She's called Xenia and she's special, frighteningly special.

He's so obsessed that he's blind to Rom's advice, to Kilroy's friendship and to the real danger that lies at the core of the Dreamcastle. A danger that could swallow him whole ... for real.

DREAMCASTLE, it's no fantasy.

DREAMCASTLE ready for access.

THINK YOU'RE UP TO IT?

UNTOUCHABLE by Eric Brown

Life might be easier for most people in 2027 but for Ana Devi, whose only home is the streets of New Delhi, it's a battle for survival. She's certainly never dreamed of visiting the bright virtual worlds of the Web. And when her brother is kidnapped the Web is certainly the last thing she is thinking about. But the Web holds the secret to what has happened to her brother and to dozens of other New Delhi street children.

How can Ana possibly find enough money to access the Web when she can barely beg enough to eat each day? Who will help her when her caste means that no one will even touch her? Somehow she must find a way or she will never see her brother again.

Dare you touch the truth of UNTOUCHABLE?

UNTOUCHABLE ready for access.

TAKE ANOTHER WALK ON THE WILD SIDE

SPIDERBITE by Graham Joyce

In 2027 a lot of schooltime is Webtime. Imagine entering Virtual Reality and creeping through the Labyrinth with the roars of the Minotaur echoing in your ears? Nowhere near as dull as the classroom. The sites are open to all, nothing is out of bounds. So why has Conrad been warned off the Labyrinth site? There shouldn't be any secrets in Edutainment.

Who is behind the savage spiders that swarm around Conrad whenever he tries to enter the site? And why do none of his friends see them? There is a dark lesson being taught at the centre of the Labyrinth ...

SPIDERBITE, school was never meant to be this scary ...

SPIDERBITE ready for access.

IS THIS THE END?

SORCERESS by Maggie Furey

A fierce and menacing intelligence is corrupting the very heart of the Web. Vital research date is being stolen. Someone or something is taking control of a spectacular new gamezone. The Web is no longer safe. The Sorceress continues to outwit all who attempt to destroy her, but her time is running out and she will stop at nothing to get what she wants. Someone must stop her.

Only one person has the power to overcome the awesome creator of the Web.

But who could survive a battle with the Sorceress?

SORCERESS ready for access shortly.